Echo Effect

Robert D. Armstrong

Sign up to Receive Free Books and $0.99 New Releases at www.enterechoeffect.com

For every new book release, I randomly select 200 mailing list subscribers to receive a free advance Kindle copy. All other subscribers will receive a special offer to purchase the book for only $0.99 on the day of release, before the price goes up to $3.99. This is not a newsletter. You will only be contacted about free books and $0.99 discounts on New Releases. Thanks again for your support!

Table of Contents

The Wild 70's

In 2070, the question of whether or not we were alone in the universe was finally answered.

In the worst way possible.

A colossal spacecraft of unknown origins exploded above our atmosphere, bombarding the planet with debris and killing hundreds of thousands. Despite the devastation, some craters contained wreckage of ultra-advanced technology, just begging to be reverse engineered. The infamous *Star Rust* race was on.

The world scrambled to gobble up what game changing scraps they could find, by any means necessary, but one reclusive Asian nation received a far larger share of Star Rust mana than any other.

Soon, the Democratic People's Republic of Korea housed the last major deposits of alien tech left to mine. Those smoldering craters outside of Pyongyang were now the most valuable real estate on the planet. With the whole world at each other's throats and all eyes on them, North Korea's paranoia was justified for once.

In 2074, North Korea struck first. With China and Russia busy hacking each other to bits over some Star Rust crumbs in Mongolia, Pyongyang focused most of their nuclear arsenal on the U.S. mainland.

Thanks to advancements in missile defense systems, many lives were saved. The so-called "Wet Firecracker

War" saw only a few thousand casualties from nuclear volleys versus potentially millions.

However, the North Koreans went back to the drawing board, and were readying a new batch of devastating weapons, promising to penetrate the American defenses.

Chapter One

"It's come down to this." Vala muttered.

She stepped through the dark, wet alleys of inner city Munich, Germany. Being a military brat, she had some experience overseas, but she was never alone. Her holographic eyeglasses were her only guide to a street address that fell deep in enemy territory.

Most people were indoors at that hour of the night. All except for the hunters.

She'd done her homework though. This part of town was Revenant territory, a low-level gothic gang. They were little more than a ragtag group of upstarts, dopers, and vandals, but dangerous in numbers nonetheless.

Her only saving grace was the acid rain, and she'd timed it just right. Her special hooded cipher mask protected her more than the Revenants' rags, allowing her safe passage. She navigated the streets with confidence, even with a bit of swagger in her stride, but it was all an act. Normally, she would never be there.

Like most major cities nowadays, facemasks were mandatory when outside. Designer brands such as Calvin Klein all had their own lines of facial filtration devices known as ciphers. Billboards littered cities with models posing in stylish ciphers that matched their outfits.

She passed by a group of linkers across the street, huddled together under a bus stop canopy. The glass roof was broken on one side and water poured through it. Vala didn't make eye contact with the technology addicts busy living in their virtual reality worlds. Out of her peripheral vision though, she couldn't help but see one of them broadcast a holo image of a thirty-foot dragon.

The image was believable and terrifying despite being fantasy. More than likely, they were using drugs as well, so the hallucinogens were intensifying their experience. One of the linkers had a seizure while the others simply laughed.

Technology had become the most addictive drug on the planet, far exceeding the war on illegal drugs during the previous century. The fixation on smart phones and videogames was just the primitive beginning. Linking allowed people to relive the old world, living out any fantasy through powerful, yet affordable VR (virtual reality) setups in every home. Holographic devices later took center stage, and the obsession intensified even further.

The hologram in Vala's eyeglasses was useful, projecting her destination just ahead. It was a rather unsuspecting shackled gate running down a long, dark alley. *Bet I could simply climb over it.* She approached the gate, looking through to see if anyone was there. She glanced to her right and left as shadowy forms darted across the alleys. The rain was letting up. The vandals were stirring.

A demented laugh erupted not far from her. It echoed off the buildings. "Let's go." she whispered.

She quickly banged on the gate, a cold chill running through her body. Drawing in a great breath, she shrieked down the alley. "Nur die Harten kommen in den Garten! Nur die Harten kommen in den Garten!"

She knew the Revenants would hear her call out, but she hoped someone behind the gate would answer first. It was a risk she had to take.

Vala shoved some loose strands of her dirty blonde hair behind her ears as she rattled off the phrase.

Only the strong survive. Her mysterious contact was quite insistent about giving the code before the guard even spotted her. Her accent was solid, not exactly local, but convincing enough. Outsiders were prime targets, so she had practiced.

A middle-aged man slowly appeared behind the gate, casually wading through the dark mist. He seemed out of place. He was attractive with thick white hair and a well-manicured beard. His clothes appeared homely and modest, yet well kept, almost like a worker in the fields from the early 2000s, but there weren't many fields around anymore. He smiled as he unlocked the gate. Vala bounced up and down on her toes nervously.

"Very well. Can I have your name?" His English held only the slightest hint of a German accent.

"V-Vala Thomas," she squeaked out, checking over her shoulder the whole time.

"Right this way." He ripped the gate open. She stepped inside quickly, almost before he could close it, then brushed up against it. The man paused, peering down at her before closing the gate.

"It's fine. You're safe now." He locked the gate and shoved his hands inside his pockets. The older gentleman's indulgent voice and relaxed shoulders were almost convincing enough to ease her anxiety.

Vala followed a couple of paces behind him through a door. He closed it behind her and locked it. This muted the haunting sounds from the dark dwelling outside. The room they entered appeared warm and comforting, like a cozy, small town doctor's waiting room. He stopped, motioning his hand toward a row of dark cherry wood chairs.

"You're okay. Have a seat. I'll be right with you," the man said, exiting the room.

Vala gawked around at the eerily peaceful setup. She paced slowly back and forth, peering around before sitting. It was quiet with very faint jazz playing in the background. She noticed the room was very tidy, and the white tile floor was spotless. It felt like a safe haven compared to the alleyways.

A few magazines littered one of the chairs. She sat down and thumbed through them while waiting, attempting to calm her nerves. The publications were all outdoorsy fishing and hunting magazines. Of course, the dates were all nearly forty years old. The first one she grabbed was *Deep Sea Digest*. She thought about driving her uncle's boat when she was in her teens. They weren't allowed to fish, but it was fun to get out on the water.

Since the 2040s, even sport fishing was illegal in most countries, thanks to generations of overfishing. Much of the world's cornerstone diet of seafood was extinct. People were forced to raise clones in gigantic farms run by government mandated corporations.

In supermarkets, those fish clones were known as Gens—Generation 1, 2, and so on. The first generations were usually horrible. They typically suffered from genetic mutations, some had extra fins, while others even had two sets of eyes. Usually, each generation lasted about three to six years before a new one was developed. However, the latest didn't always equal greatest, and in some generations, cost effectiveness was more important, sacrificing quality.

She sighed at the faces of the fishermen in the magazine. They looked happy. She wondered if they even had a clue that their children wouldn't be afforded the same luxury as them. Something as simple and inherently human as fishing would be gone forever. Even the sky behind the fishermen looked different then—clear, vibrant, unassuming.

Vala tossed it aside and gazed at a thirty-seven-year-old wildlife magazine. She'd seen videos online of elephants, but now she wondered what it was like seeing those last wild elephants in real life. The title of the main article was "Goodbye, Old Friends" featuring the last seven wild elephants on Earth.

A billionaire name Simeon Bullock hired a team of mercenaries to protect those last few for several years. To his credit, he spent millions of dollars trying to sustain them. It worked for a while, but the ivory soon became too expensive until the elephants were betrayed by their own guardians. All slaughtered for a bit of ivory, silencing them forever. Elephant clones were introduced later, but they all had genetic defects, namely weak hearts and joints.

"Vala?" A man startled her as she put down the magazine. "Oh, yes." She scrambled to her feet.

"Those magazines are a bit out of date, yes? I like to remember those days." This time, it was a younger man, dressed like a doctor in a lab coat, that greeted her. He was the same height, but he had pale skin and dark hair.

"Come on back." He flicked a well-manicured hand towards some side door while never taking his eyes off his holochart. They strolled down the sterile and too quiet hall until she couldn't bear the silence any longer.

"So…it's just the two of you here?" she asked.

"No, it's just me at this facility," he hummed in a comforting voice far too old for him.

"But..." Vala squinted, recognizing his voice from before. It was the same as the old man.

Cilans. Genetic mimicry masters. It was said there were less than thirty in the entire world. She paused for a moment then took a big gulp.

He guided her to a small lab area with a large dentist-like chair. "Have a seat," he calmly said, walking over to the counter and rummaging through a cabinet.

Vala sat down and attempted not to stare at the man, but he just seemed so different from before. Everything about his altered physical features appeared so natural and convincing.

There was a long pause. He studied the ceiling, placing his hands on his hips and sighed.

"So, Vala. I'm curious, and I have to ask, what exactly would make you want to go through with this procedure? You seem like a nice, intelligent young woman. Is it for Star Rust contacts? Ego? You have to understand, the people that usually come to me are much...*different*," he said, shrugging his shoulders.

"Different in what way?" She twirled the loose string from her jacket. Her foot shook as she planted down her weight, stopping it.

"Mercenary companies with a lot of cash, mostly. They've sent over some of their people... I've had a couple celebrities and an aging Brazilian supermodel recently," he said.

"I'm looking for someone." He studied her with a slightly puzzled look. He turned back around and washed his hands. Then, he arranged a set of vials on a tray.

"That's a first. *Well*, actually second then... Now, I'm a businessman first and foremost, so pushing you away is not good business for me. It doesn't make sense, right?" he said with a smile.

"Not really, no. I'm paying you good money." She cut her eyes at him.

"So having said that, I will still say this. With the money you're spending with *me*, you could hire some of the best trackers on the planet and save yourself a lot of pain," he said.

"Trackers can't get inside where I need to be... What kind of pain are we talking?"

"Well, to start, about 8% don't survive this initial operation. Then, an additional 13% die within the first year. If you survive that you're looking at a mid-fifties lifespan at best. This procedure, which you're paying a hefty price for, is incredibly taxing on the human body," he said in a serious tone raising his eyebrows.

"I have a rare genetic degenerative spinal condition, so quality of later life isn't my concern." Vala said.

"Did you consider using your heap of cash for experimental treatment possibly?" he glared at her.

"That was the plan originally. Not anymore. Listen. What will this transformation allow me to do exactly? I know the general idea, altering skin and hair colors, but I want to hear the details," she said.

"Well. Ok. Yes, of course. One moment," the doctor said. He walked around and arranged some of the vials on a tray beside her chair. They were different colors—some very bright, almost neon. He wheeled forward a chest-high machine with tubes draped around it and began unwrapping the hoses.

He pressed a button, then a tanning bed-sized structure cascaded from the wall with a reflective surface. A hatch opened on the side of the metallic, shiny cocoon. Vala squirmed while the Cilan calmly prepared the life-altering procedure.

She stared at herself in the reflection, "At least I can hide my freckles." She only had a few dots below her dark green eyes, sprinkled evenly about on her smooth olive skin. Her lips were full and her nose pointed up a little more than she liked. She didn't like people staring at her nostrils.

"Well, first you'll have increased reflexes and awareness to start. It'll send your muscle fibers into a stronger state, much like humans from twenty to thirty thousand years ago. You'll be faster and have more physical endurance."

"How long does all this take?" she asked.

"About four to six weeks. You'll be completely down for the first week. Then, the obvious skin, eye, and hair alterations will begin to surface by the third week. Those can be changed on the fly. With training, you can alter the color of any organic tissue on your body within seconds. You can look older or younger than you are, if you wish, and even a different race in many cases," he said.

"I'm guessing the Brazilian model didn't come here to look older?" She laughed just a little too hard.

"No." He chuckled.

Anxiety glued Vala to her seat. The stale statistical odds jumped out and seized her throat.

"So will I be awake during this?"

"Yes. The first four days are the fun part. Basically, I'm going to saturate your entire body with a host of unregulated chemicals, which fill your pores with cancer-causing serums. It can best be described as burning. Everywhere you have skin, you will feel a burning sensation during the skin treatment. You can't move and there is no relief. I can't sedate you either or your heart will stop," he said casually.

"Is that how patients die? Cancer?"

"Some of them. The problem is your body will be more resilient in many ways, so this slows the disease, and death. Imagine a champion horse with cancer. He'll fight it a bit longer, but the end result is the same usually."

"Ohhhh—my—God." Vala slammed her hands over her face. Fighting back the tears, she gulped and counted to ten. She knew Michael wouldn't want her to do this.

He stopped his preparations, genuine concern on his face. "Vala, are you *sure*? I can't stop it once it starts," he said.

She closed her eyes and muttered "Michael..." She was already dying on the inside.

"Y-Yes," she stuttered. After a moment's pause, she summoned the courage to continue.

The doctor stared at her, clucking his tongue. "Positive?"

She set her jaw and locked eyes with him. "I'm sure."

He tucked his hands down into his lab coat pockets and wagged his head slowly. "There is only one thing I can imagine that would make a normal human being subject themselves to, *this* type of torture. I felt it once..."

He paused for a moment, examining his shoes. "Even though it has been a long time. I... remember." He grinned and his gaze drifted off to some faraway place.

"What would make a normal person do this?" Vala asked.

"Love..." the doctor said.

Vala dropped her head slightly and glanced away, uncomfortable that the doctor could see her intentions so clearly.

"The army... They lied to me about him. I'm going to find out what happened. That's why normal trackers won't touch it. This is a military-related contract." She spit out the final words. Her eyes watered as she sat up straight despite the stresses that surrounded her.

"I'm very sorry to hear that. Well, Cilans like myself are in high demand for Star Rust contracts. Everyone wants those alien materials now more than ever. Delivery, stealing, whatever... Just get out there and get your name known. It's all about favors. Maybe this could get your foot in the door so you could find information."

"Possibly."

"Yes, dear. *Possibly*. Once I turn this machine on, there are no guarantees that you'll wake up. It's possible you won't," he said.

"We've gone over that." She gave him an arctic glare.

"Assuming you survive, we'll train you the best we can. That's part of the package you paid for. Reconnaissance. Weapons handling. Your physical abilities will put you a cut above your average hired gun, but training is very important. Be sure to go through all the virtual reality modules. Those will take twelve to sixteen weeks. After that, you're on your own."

Vala tapped her foot. She wanted to ask a question, but she found it difficult to word without being offensive.

"How did...you... Why did you—" Vala started, gesturing at him.

"Ah, yes... My reasons... Well, my operation was very personal as well, but not quite as heroic as your situation. Let's just say I was heartbroken, and I acted out of desperation. Hmm. Maybe I thought being someone else could get back the one I loved. Looking back, it was the worst decision I ever made," he said in a low tone with his head down.

After a long moment, he cleared his throat. "Still willing to go ahead with it?"

"Let's do it," Vala said, hiding her shaking hands behind her back. *I have to find Michael, I know he's out there...*

Chapter Two

Several weeks earlier…

"Four minutes!" Lieutenant Wheeler barked back into the helicopter at Michael and his Ranger strike team. If any were nervous, they hid it well. They had done this dozens of times. Some of them appeared like factory workers on an assembly line as they checked each other's gear.

"Any changes from the intelligence report on troop strength, sir?" Michael asked. Even though the lieutenant was technically in command, the men looked to Michael for leadership.

"Still looks like about the same, ninety strong. No activity around the LZ though. Should be a quiet insertion." Wheeler kept his face buried in his tablet.

"Should be." Michael whispered to himself. He'd heard that before.

Michael was tall, standing generously above six feet. His shoulders were broad and remarkably robust sitting atop an otherwise lean swimmer's shape. To any onlooker, it was obvious Michael was built for power and speed. A lethal and necessary combination in Michael's line of work. His perfectly symmetrical dark eyes were brown under most conditions, but when the light hit them just right, a touch of amber glowed around his pupils. They shined above his all-American jaw line revealing a deep sense of purpose that commanded his team's unwavering allegiance.

As the quadcopter nearly brushed the treetops, Michael's legs swayed back and forth below the open door. The cool night sky prickled his heated skin. He raised his night vision and stared off into the mountainous North Korean wilderness, deceptively peaceful in the moonlight. It didn't look much different from his native state of Alaska, not at night anyway.

"Hey, Mike, you *are* going home after this one, right?" Sergeant Daniel Naben clicked in over the inter-squad radio. He flashed his trademarked goofy smile around his gapped front teeth.

"One way or the other," Michael responded casually.

"Well, let's hope it isn't the *other* way. I got your back."

"That's what I'm afraid of." Michael grinned. Daniel laughed, stepping across the chopper beside Michael.

"Ah, you'll be with her in less than a week." Daniel said, patting him on the shoulder.

"That's what they told me three weeks ago." Michael rolled his eyes.

"That's the Army for ya. How is she doing? Any word?" Daniel asked. Michael's fiancé, Vala, had recently been diagnosed with an unknown mutation of spinal muscular atrophy. Years of military budget cuts eventually halted experimental medical coverage for undocumented diseases, including Vala's.

"We just found a doctor that has a plan for treatment. It's extremely expensive, but he seems confident at least." he replied.

"Great news."

"Yeah, the doctors on base referred me to him, we're going together to start treatment when I get back." Michael said.

"Leaving one war to fight another." Daniel said.

"Looks that way." Michael said raising an eyebrow. His mission was to sell the house his dad willed to him for a down payment on her treatment. But since he was in a war zone, he needed a backup plan in case he didn't make it back. He'd secretly qualified for a military contract that promised a designated beneficiary a massive payout, enough to undergo Vala's treatment.

The requirements for the contract were that Michael have extensive combat experience and be in the top five percent of aptitude marks, focusing on intelligence and decision making. The other stipulation was that the military science division would take possession of his body if he was killed or severely injured.

"I know it's easier said than done, but let's handle tonight first, we need you with a clear head." Daniel said.

"One step at a time." Michael replied. The thing is he'd been doing the opposite. During the night, he was a Ranger serving on combat missions, but during the day he was a researcher combing through medical journals and making phone calls to doctors.

Michael had also been on more combat missions than any other Ranger in his outfit. Not because he volunteered, but because his superiors wanted him out there. He was *that* guy. The one that got things done.

"One minute!" Wheeler spouted. The all-electric whirlybirds barely muffled his nasally voice.

Michael stood up and circled a finger over his head at the twelve men he'd served with for the last several months. He met each of their eyes for a split second as he grabbed the rope, preparing to rappel down into the darkness.

With a deep breath, he inhaled the chilled air and held it for a moment before exhaling. He checked his weapon for the fourth time.

Beside him, Sgt. Daniel Naben glanced down and snickered at Michael's dated gun. He was one of only two Rangers in his unit still using a projectile-based firearm, whereas most everyone else had upgraded to laser-based weaponry.

Daniel powered up his sleek, plastic laser. "I'm surprised you don't have a sword too. Stay away from my head this time. That thing is kinda loud."

Michael just shrugged. It was an unusual characteristic, considering most Ranger units carried the same weapons. However, Michael felt a connection with the projectile weapons, he liked the raw feedback and recoil. The relationship was solidified in his youth, growing up around guns and wildlife in the Alaskan woodlands. He fired his first rifle at six years old, barely strong enough to hold it correctly. Much like his dated weapon, Michael likened himself to men of old, specifically WWII. He admired their grit and self-sacrificing ambition to serve.

Wheeler chimed in over the radio. "Remember, men, this is just armed recon. If there's a nuke here, we secure the area and let our robot friend EVE work her magic. If the target's too heavily defended, we back off and shadow them. Don't force the enemy into a 'use it or lose it' scenario. No hero shit. Our priority, as always, is making sure they can't ever point that thing towards home."

"Don't see why we can't just call in an airstrike. Wham, bam, thank you, ma'am." Daniel threw up his hands with a whispered *kaboom*.

"Because the Koreans aren't exactly known for their quality construction. As much as I'd like to blast the fucking thing to hell, we can't risk an accidental detonation. All those civvies, they don't deserve it." The North Korean army had strategically placed warheads near their civilian populations, so even the slightest risk of detonation wasn't an option.

Michael looped the rappelling rope in his hand, yanking on it tightly as he listened to Wheeler. He was a new commander, a "butter bar" as they called the twin golden bars marking a second lieutenant. Generally, a more senior commander should be running this type of high-priority op.

With so many thousands of suspected nuclear sites to inspect though, there just weren't enough big dogs to go around.

Wheeler at least seemed confident, despite his inexperience. Some said he was former enlisted, but that didn't matter much to Michael. All he cared about was his men, his country, and getting home to Vala who desperately needed him. Time wasn't on her side.

"Twenty seconds!"

The Rangers looked toward Michael while spot-checking their gear as the stealth chopper reached its drop altitude. They knew the drill. As thrilling as this first taste of combat seemed for the new commander, he had no idea what these men had already been through.

"Rope out! Go! Go! Go!" Michael slid down the swinging snake first. He shot down the rope as the green exterior light faded on the tree next to him, slowly dissipating into the blackness as he reached the bottom.

He landed with a thud, dashed forward to the nearest tree and flicked his rifle up. A holographic visor dropped from his helmet, the tactical display filling up with green dots in seconds. He cycled to a perfect combination of night vision and infrared until he could see even better than in broad daylight. He could already detect several small rodents in the distance, but no humans.

As soon as the last Ranger's boots hit the ground the chopper flittered off. The crew would fly around for the next hour doing fake touch and go insertions to confuse the enemy.

"Everyone good?" Michael questioned, checking an interface tab on his visor that displayed the condition of each of his team members.

"We're solid, Staff Sergeant," Daniel confirmed.

"Alright. Everyone on me. Wedge formation, but mind your spacing. These bastards love their booby traps. The target is about 800 meters out. Let's make Butter Bars look good," Michael ordered.

"Um, you know he can hear you, right?" Daniel snickered in his squad comm.

"Of course I do. No offense, sir." Michael glanced back at Wheeler and smiled. Daniel shook his head. "You don't want to ever go home, do you?"

"Butch, any radiation?" Michael asked before they got too deep. Even though most of the nuclear missiles were shot down in the first war, radiation blanketed the atmosphere and tended to float down in the weirdest places.

"Some hot spots here and there, but tolerable while we're here. Unless you guys wanna build a bonfire or something, maybe hang out?" Butch shrugged, scanning a device on his wrist.

"Ha, yeah, speaking of bonfires. You guys remember the one at Mike's that almost burnt down his house?" Daniel said.

"I do," Michael chuckled while they marched.

"Barely. I had a few too many *beverages*, but I do remember Vala kicking everyone out. Kinda frightening actually, with the yelling and all, but then I realized she weighs less than my thigh," Butch replied.

"You still woulda had your hands full." Michael shook his head, glancing over at Butch.

"Probably. How's she doing anyway?" Butch asked.

"No symptoms yet, but I need to get back to her." Michael replied. He squinted his eyes, glancing down at the ground for a moment. He thought about her original diagnosis and when she would begin to see indicators. He understood the risks. Vala could lose control of her motor skills at any time and be bound to a wheelchair, bedridden, or worse.

Michael had a strategy in place for when he got back to the states to pay for her treatment. Along with selling his home, he had better than average credit for a medical loan. He'd also been saving his money, considering he had little expenses on deployment. Michael figured if he could piece it all together, they'd have a chance to afford the rounds of nanobot surgery and medication.

"Understandable Mike." Butch nodded.

Butch was the technical guru, a burly man with a perfectly manicured, unauthorized black beard. No one really knew if the nickname was because his stepdad was an actual meat butcher or some other reason. There were a few bets on its origin, but no winners.

"Alright, let's cut the chatter. Lip sync only," Michael ordered. Lip sync was a nifty option. A small device on the Ranger's chinstrap could interpret individual mouth movements so accurately it would translate to audio inside the other soldier's earpieces while maintaining total silence.

"You know, my wife hates when we use lip syncing on missions..." Butch moved his lips as his voice was perfectly simulated throughout their helmets.

"Why?" Daniel asked.

"Because when we talk afterwards, I'm *still* lip syncing. Anyone else do that?" Butch asked.

"Yep, Vala notices it too. She thought I was singing a..."

Michael and the team flopped to the ground reflexively as a tactical warning light flashed in every Ranger's visor.

"Sensor drone, 10 O'clock, 140 meters," Butch said.

The mobile little scouts used a sound-based radar that could detect human heartbeats out to a kilometer.

"Our torso damper is near 90%. I'm surprised it can detect our heart rates so far away," Daniel said.

"Stay put," Michael mouthed. He raised up in a crouch and hurried about sixty paces away from the unit. He slid behind a large tree, putting it between himself and the drone.

"Staff Sergeant?" Wheeler blinked as Michael snapped off part of his torso damper, baiting the drone in.

"Guys, this is a pretty beefy drone with two minigun laser turrets on deck," Butch said.

The robot veered towards Michael's position, spooling up its turrets in anticipation. Michael leaned around the tree and drew a bead on the dark vessel. The metallic spherical drone bobbed up and down like a blowfish as it hovered through the misty forest.

"That thing is thirty meters from you," Daniel said as all the Rangers drew their weapons on the drone. "Just give the order, Mike."

"Mike?"

"Fifteen meters…"

"Hold," Michael ordered, signaling them to stay low.

As the drone approached the large tree, it circled cautiously first, but Michael shuffled around the trunk. The drone slowly orbited the tree behind Michael just far enough to point its weapons away from Michael's men, completely giving the Rangers its backside.

"Fire!"

The Rangers pelted the attack drone with a merciless barrage of laser fire, cutting it to pieces and scorching the tree Michael was hiding behind, setting the bark on fire. The drone crumpled to the ground in a pile of smoke and debris.

"Target down." Daniel sighed as Michael fled from behind the burning tree. Butch smiled as he ran out, scratching his beard.

"MT-SOL978 attack drone. Only weak point is its backside. Cute but kinda risky, Mike. That drone could have ripped through the tree if it wanted to," Butch said.

"It should have. *Artificial* intelligence at its best. Probably needed confirmation on a target first." Michael adjusted his torso damper under his body armor. "We've got only minutes before they send out another one to inspect, or worse. Follow me!" He waved his men on toward the main objective.

The Rangers raced after him, swiftly pushing toward the objective, sacrificing stealth for speed. After a few minutes, Michael could see the target installation surrounded by a double-layered chain link fence.

Daniel adjusted the settings on his laser and sliced open the fence with a flick of his wrist. While the team filed through, Michael ordered four Rangers to stay behind, stalking the perimeter as snipers.

"I'm dialed in on their network. Picking up alert chatter on their comms. They're suspicious about why that drone isn't responding," Butch said.

"I know. Follow me," Michael replied. He used his visor's holographic display to help him navigate through the installation, most of which was filled with cargo and transport vehicles. They stayed close, pushing through sets of dark, twenty-meter-long cargo bins for cover and flanking wide around the nuclear warhead.

"They're at full alert now. Must have found the destroyed drone," Butch said. About that time, an alarm blared above them.

"Dammit. Maybe we shoulda did the bonfire." Daniel mumbled.

"We've come this far. There's no backing out now," Michael said as his eyelid quivered under the stress. They could hear men giving orders and boots pounding the pavement all around them. The sounds came from the direction of the downed drone.

Butch buried his face in his tablet. The holographic display illuminated his face with a light blue tint as his eyes skipped toward Michael. "I'm picking up a steady hotspot. Warhead must be through this next set of cargo bins and on the other side of an armored flatbed truck. Here. Looks like they were about to load it up for transport. We have three guards protecting it." Butch explained, showing Michael on his tablet.

"Warhead assembled?" Wheeler jumped in.

"Umm. Let's see, zooming in…Negative, we can open fire, but I'd play it safe though, grenades or explosions are not recommended as usual."

"Let's get it done," Michael said. Wheeler cut his eyes at Michael, but nodded his head in agreement.

They pushed through the next set of cargo bins, climbing over boxes of ammunition, drone parts, and explosives in the process. Just outside the cargo bin door was their objective.

"On my command, other side of this door, standard breach and clear, three targets within fifteen meters. Hit 'em hard and fast…" Michael led with his team stacked close behind him. He gripped the aluminum door handle with his hand.

He thought about Vala at home, then he glared back at his men and nodded. So many people back home were counting on him. He felt the pressure resonating around his neck as Daniel patted him on the back. "Ready."

Michael slammed the door open as they fanned out with guns blazing.

Michael's rifle boomed over his team's zinging laser weapons. They dropped all three targets instantly. Two of them had their backs to the Rangers while the last one didn't even have time to raise his weapon. The blaring alarm assisted the breach, dampening the chaos of the takedown.

"Clear!" Daniel said.

"Clear, all targets," Butch confirmed.

"Butch, get Eve on it… *Now*," Lieutenant Wheeler ordered.

"Done." Butch unstrapped his satchel and pulled out a compact drone named Eve. From the drone, a set of four bipedal twiggy legs retracted, making her about knee high. Eve was their explosives expert. Her body was shaped like a small metal dog, but had a round, light blue sphere for a head. Her front arms sported human-like hands with six long fingers.

Eve trotted over to the warhead sealed inside a metal container. The container was about the size of a trunk storage in a full-sized car. Eve appeared excited, like a dog that had found a treat. She looked back up at Butch for approval as her antenna tail wagged back and forth.

"We've already found it for you, Eve. Get after it," Butch ordered as the rest of the Rangers stood watch.

Eve's left hand flattened and morphed into a circular saw spinning at high velocity. It made a sound similar to a chainsaw, but a miniature, muffled version. She cut through the metal bands and locks around the container to open it. Sparks flew up into the air as she ripped through the seals.

"Come on, Eve." Michael checked his men, all taking a knee in an outward facing circle from the bomb. No jokes, no more chatter. Their eyes bounced around at all the possible ambush points. This was not an easy position to defend. It was cluttered with cargo boxes and had multiple entrances.

As she broke the last seal, the top lid of the container popped loose. The Rangers opened the heavy container, revealing a complex array of holographic instruments around a roadside cone sized warhead.

"Amazing these little shits can kill a billion people," Daniel said under his breath.

"This one won't. We'll defend from the back of the truck. Let Eve work her magic, and we'll wait here to make sure the job's done," Michael said. The Rangers hopped up into the back of the flatbed, overlooking the warhead through the shooting slots in the armored canopy.

"Good idea," Daniel agreed.

Just before Eve started working, she projected a fake holographic image throughout her body. The hologram displayed a North Korean guard dog, complete with an authentic collar and emblems.

"Whoa," Michael said, glaring at Butch.

"That's a cool trick, but it's not going to fool anyone if they come over here," Daniel said, criticizing Eve's tactic. "Why on earth would a guard dog be standing over an exposed nuclear warhead like that?"

"It's bizarre enough to make someone stop and think for a second, which gives us time to react," Butch replied.

"Hostiles approaching Eve to her left. Again, hostiles approaching." Butch finally took his eyes off of the computer.

"I should have kept my damn mouth shut," Daniel said, rolling his eyes.

Suddenly, two guards stormed the warhead with their guns drawn. They froze at the sight their dead comrades littered about, then the "guard dog" perched over the warhead. Eve turned around, facing them before sitting down. Her hologram even *looked* guilty, like walking in on a dog that had torn the sofa to shreds.

The soldiers shuffled about aimlessly. One of them attempted to push Eve away from the warhead with his foot. "Move!" the soldier bellowed in Korean.

When he made contact, his foot tapped metal, not fur, and the image of the guard dog flickered.

"Fire!" Michael led by example.

Eve darted between his legs as the Rangers lit them up with invisible and silent laser strikes. One of the dying men pulled his weapon's trigger as he fell. The loud, unsilenced gunshot from the fallen North Korean echoed throughout the compound. It was far louder than even Michael's weapon.

"Shit! We can't stay here. We need to extract, Sergeant." Wheeler scrambled to his feet.

"Status?" Michael asked.

"Eve's at 62%," Butch said.

"Hey, the truck they're using to transport. Can you drive this thing, Daniel?"

"I'll figure it out. You just watch out for the cops!" Daniel joked as he punched buttons until the engine roared to life. "Easy enough."

"Pull the truck up next to the warhead, Daniel. Butch, load Eve up in the back. We gotta ride," Michael ordered.

Daniel pulled forward as four Rangers surrounded the container. They hoisted it up swiftly and carefully, sliding it into the bed of the truck while the other Rangers defended the entrances. Eve jumped into the bed of the truck effortlessly.

"Sergeant, lots more hostiles approaching. At least twenty, judging by the comm chatter," Wheeler said excitedly. The remaining Rangers piled into the back of the truck, each taking a firing position from the bed, covering every angle.

The path ahead was clear of obstacles, minus the small detail of the front gate's concrete barricade. "Go! We're all in! I called the bird in. It's five minutes out." Wheeler rattled.

"This should be fun..." Daniel smashed the accelerator. As he took off, enemy rounds pounded the transport truck. Some must have been armor piercing as they gouged holes throughout the cabin. Daniel winced and grabbed his shoulder. "Arrgghhh! Shit, that burns!"

"You need me to take over?!" Michael slapped a self-adhesive field dressing on him. The exotic composite material sealed the wound and applied pressure as needed, even releasing a topical anesthetic to dull the pain.

"Nah... I got it!" Daniel kept both hands on the wheel somehow. Eve resumed disarming the nuke as the Rangers returned fire all around her.

"Great job, but don't slow down!" Wheeler bellowed from the backseat.

"Left side, seven hostiles," one of the Rangers whistled over his buzzing laser rifle.

"Six...five...hostiles. Now three," Butch replied as the Ranger's suppressive fire mowed the field. Daniel mashed the accelerator, barreling toward the gate as gunfire erupted back and forth.

"Tank!" Daniel yanked the wheel just as an armored turret popped out from behind a storage container.

The tank fired at point blank range, narrowly missing them. It was too close to swivel its turret, but the force jarred the Rangers' vehicle. It rolled on two wheels for a moment before slamming back down, dust ejected from the impact before leveling out.

"Y'all want to take it easy up there? Don't wake the baby!" Butch waved his tablet at the ripped open nuke.

"Damn backseat drivers..." Daniel hit 40mph just before reaching the gate, but he sideswiped a parked Jeep attempting to evade the tank, knocking it aside. Enemy soldiers at the gate ran and jumped out of the way. Some seemed confused by the scene. That *was* their truck just moments ago. The Rangers ping-ponged through a set of barricades before straightening up, all while taking and returning fire.

"Keep going. Get away from that damn tank! Don't drive in a straight line. Zig zag!" Michael ordered. He swung back to Eve and laughed at her latest holo projection. "Why the turtle, Butch?"

"Uhhh, this bumpy road is slowing her down. Maybe she can't work as fast? She might be telling us to find a smooth surface," Butch replied. A couple of the Rangers chuckled, but one of them started coughing.

A wet, warm cough.

One of the Rangers slumped down, but kept his weapon trained out of his damaged firing port.

"Sergeant Clements!" The team medic bounded across the flatbed and laid Clements out straight. Clements was one of the older Rangers, the silent type. A family man.

"Ahh, whatda we got? Um, let's see. Small laser scorn in the chest cavity. No problem." Despite his cheery tone, he shot Michael a grim glare while Clements slipped out of consciousness.

Michael almost cursed aloud, but he held it in, scanning the men around him.

He'd been in this position before in combat. It didn't get easier, but he understood now wasn't the time to get upset.

Lieutenant Wheeler tapped the mic on his shoulder. "Snipers, break contact and head to the extraction site. I have a chopper headed this way."

"Mike! That tank... It's moving on us...fast. It's a blister tank..." Butch muttered. Blister tanks were known for their straight-line speed.

No way to outrun one in a cargo truck.

"Eve?"

"She's at 93%... It's the road. It's too bumpy..." Butch said, observing the mountainous portion of the terrain.

Michael had to think fast. That tank crew probably had no idea they were chasing the warhead, so they were coming for blood. A direct hit could set off the nuke. Not only was Michael concerned for his men, but for all the civilians nearby.

Wheeler took a deep breath. "All right... Daniel, slow down. Everyone is getting off this truck now, except me and Eve. We'll regroup later, but I—"

"I thought you said no hero shit, sir. No one's leaving you behind." Michael barked as several of the other Rangers voiced their agreement.

"Sergeant, that's not an option. It's an order. Off this truck. Now. I appreciate everyone's loyalty, but this is not about that. This is about saving lives. The lot of you are weighing this vehicle down. I need as much speed as possible." Michael cocked an eyebrow in newfound respect for the LT. Deep down, Michael didn't think the extra weight mattered much, but Wheeler needed to find a way to get them out of the vehicle.

"Tank will be within range in fifty seconds, Mike," Butch said, glancing down at his tablet.

"Everyone, file out and get off the road. Stay low. That tank won't care about anything other than this truck. Get to the extraction zone the snipers have set up. Once you get onboard, have that pilot haul ass out of here. Go!" Wheeler started shoving troops as Daniel hit the brakes.

Michael grunted at the Rangers, all still refusing to budge. "You heard the lieutenant. An order is an order."

Everyone stepped off, except for Michael, Wheeler, and Daniel. He struggled to heft Clements's lifeless corpse over the side to the waiting Rangers.

"Give me a hand, sir?"

As soon as Wheeler grabbed Clements's feet, Michael released the body. "Sorry sir, can't let you do it." With one smooth motion, Michael kicked the LT in his armored vest, knocking both men over the side. Michael shook his head as he watched Wheeler tumble a few times before standing up slowly.

"Go!" Michael yelled at Daniel in the cab.

"Shit. How far along is Eve?" Daniel asked.

"97%"

Suddenly, a streak of light flew over the truck, momentarily lighting up the entire wilderness. It was immediately followed by a thunderous boom in the distance.

"That's getting close." Michael said.

"I know. Maybe slide the nuke container closer so we can watch Eve from up here." Daniel said.

Michael dragged the box as far as he could and plopped down in the passenger seat. He glared over at Daniel. "Now it's your turn."

"For what?" Daniel asked.

"To get out. Do I have to knock you out first?"

"Ahhh…you know, I figured out another reason why you needed to get back to Vala in a hurry…" Daniel sighed, looking in his rearview mirror.

"Yeah?"

"Because you would die for us out here if it came down to it." Daniel shook his head. "This was supposed to be your last one, man."

"Daniel, I'm going home too, I need this warhead disarmed. Regroup with the guys and get them out of here. The LT needs someone to keep him grounded. He's a good dude, but lacks experience."

"No talking you outta this?" Daniel asked. He dropped his head and opened the door.

"Nope. Watch that shoulder." Michael took over the wheel. Daniel punched his arm. "I won't forget this."

He tucked and rolled without another word. Michael watched him in his side view mirror. He hurried off the road, just as he was ordered.

"Good luck, buddy. You'll need—"

A blast right behind the back wheel lifted the truck. Shrapnel bounced off his helmet and armored back as the truck slammed sideways into a guardrail. The truck skidded down the steel rail as sparks flew into the air.

"Damn!" Michael regained control. He glanced at the mirror and saw the tank was only about 500 meters away and approaching fast.

He spun around to check Eve's status, but she wasn't there. The container had been slung up against the side of the truck and was propped on its side.

"EVE!?"

He scanned ahead to get a visual on the road. It appeared to be straight with no curves. He wedged his rifle between the throttle and the seat and let off the steering wheel slowly, gauging to see if it would hold a line. "Come on!"

Michael darted back to the bed of the truck. "Eve, dammit. Where the hell—"

His eyes scanned all around, but she was nowhere to be found. Then he spotted the missing tail gate. "Oh no... She was thrown out."

Michael ran over to the nuke, and surprisingly, it had already been disarmed.

"She did it…"

A rush of heat filled his body as a shockwave flung him up. His helmet smashed against the armored truck roof, rupturing his eardrums with a screeching rip. For a moment, time seemed to stop. He was floating, gazing out at the stars in the night sky from the rear gate of the truck. Then, suddenly, something crushed his upper back and then his side.

The tank had landed a round just behind the truck, flipping it end over end. It felt like being in a giant washing machine. Michael eventually opened his eyes, but he couldn't keep them open. He was blacking out.

He tried to stand, but neither leg would so much as twitch. North Korean voices chirped around him. "Vala…she…needs me…"

A rifle butt slammed into Michael's temple as he reached for his sidearm, knocking him unconscious. He went into a deep sleep, reliving the last time he'd seen her.

"Everything ready? Your unit's flight leaves in forty minutes." Vala stamped her foot and peeked over the mountain of bulging duffel bags. She tugged at her blonde hair, nearly ripping them out by the purple roots, and fiddled with the fraying tips.

Michael kept his broad back to her, as he'd done all day, and snapped the case shut on an ancient 9mm Berretta. The expensive and carefully maintained pistol was full of moving parts.

"I guess so. Seems like every time I come home on leave, I cram a year's worth of shopping into a month. You know..."

"So tell me again, what would happen if you just didn't go to North Korea?" Vala smirked.

"Let's see, desertion during war time? We're looking at five years in prison and a dishonorable discharge realistically."

"You've actually considered it. Wow. I could tell by your tone and how fast you rattled that off." Vala suspected.

"For a split second, yeah. It's an irrational thought though. But it boils my blood the Army won't cover your treatment, even after we get married." Michael explained.

He clammed up and scratched his short, dark hair while grinding his teeth to nubs. He pressed his Army dress blues in last. Vala glided over, squeezing Michael's hand and pressing it against his chest.

"It falls under 'research' they say. In other words, it could cost them millions." Vala mumbled.

"Ridiculous."

Michael glanced over at the full body mirror of them embracing one another. They were a young couple, each twenty-six years old. Michael stared at the scars on his thick, muscular forearms as Vala caressed her fingers up and down them.

He drank in her scent while gently pushing her off. "We're running short on time, let's load up."

"Ok. If you've left anything behind, I'll have to take up a second job so I can ship it to North Korea." Vala grinned and hefted one of his bags with both hands, but could only drag it across the room.

"Wait, you had a first job!?" Michael spun around, smirking.

"Funny. If EBay puts the bacon on the table, then EBay it is. Matter of fact, if you do leave anything here of value maybe I'll just—"

"Haha, yeah," Michael smiled. He stepped in, pecking her with a kiss on the lips. "Please just don't sell Uncle Sam's stuff, Vala."

"Please don't get my fiancé hurt, Uncle Sam," Vala said under her breath.

Michael shut the rear gate to his SUV. Vala was already waiting for him in the passenger seat. With her knees pointed towards the drivers side, her green eyes tracked his every move as he came around and got in. Michael felt like she was soaking up everything she could, she knew he could be gone a long while.

Vala flipped down the sun visor and opened up the mirror, briefly checking what little makeup she had on.

"So, not to bring up the worst case scenario here, but what if I start showing symptoms while you're deployed?" Vala asked. Michael sighed.

"For now, we stick to the plan." He stared off into the horizon casting an orange tint across the San Diego suburbs. The light reflected off the windows of twin high rises on both sides of the road, creating an illuminated arch effect as they approached.

"I'm dedicating my life to solving this problem," Michael said.

"I know, but you heard the doctor. He said it could be two weeks or two years before my symptoms show up. They just know so little about it, that's what makes it terrifying." She said.

"The doctor's diagnosis has been playing on repeat in my mind for weeks." He said.

"God forbid what if something happens to you while you're over there?" she asked.

"Nothing will happen. I'm coming back and we're tackling this, together." Michael said looking away. He bit his lip.

"Just be realistic. You don't know that, Mike. Do you think Mrs. Chandler next door expected to see that Army priest? We watched her, do you remember that haunting sound she made on her front porch when she found out about her husband? I do. I never thought I'd get a disease that could paralyze, even kill me either. It's just how life goes."

Michael pulled over his SUV, throwing it in park. He turned on his emergency flashers, then stared forward. "You know me. You know us." He turned towards her.

"I do. I just—"

"I keep going back to what we went through with my dad." Michael lowered his voice, staring straight ahead.

"The addiction?"

"Remember what the doctors said?" Michael asked.

"I remember it was grim."

"They said they'd never seen such a powerful addiction, Vala. Ever. These were doctors that dealt with technology addiction daily. Dad was speaking to fake hologram characters, but in reality. He didn't even know us Vala."

"I know."

"We worked together and put our lives on hold to help him. We grew as a team. We taught him how to live again." Michael said. Neither of them said a word for several seconds.

"The vacancy in his eyes in the beginning, that was scary. Then one day I remember seeing a small spark when he started remembering us. It really was beautiful. From there on, he just got better and better." She recalled.

"Why do you think he made such a drastic improvement after that?" Michael asked.

"I think, he had something to fight for then," she said.

Michael glared over at her, nodding his head slowly. "While I'm over there, I'll continue to work on this. We do what we talked about. We research, we pray, we do everything in our power. It's not an ideal situation with me deployed, but we play the hand we're dealt. You continue talking to the doctors and I'll try and find alternate forms of treatment until I get back. There is an answer, we just need to find it."

"Michael... Mike... Mike. Wake up!" Daniel nudged him. Michael rose off the concrete floor, using the prison bars to stand. "What, where?! Oh no." He looked around, his eyes were wide, but then he grabbed his back in pain. "Aahhhh-hhhhh! This isn't happening. Daniel we have to get home man, Vala—"

"Keep it down. They're right outside," Daniel whispered, putting his hand over Michael's mouth.

"Listen, Mike. We have to find a way out of here. The longer we're here, you know the worse our chances are."

"Dammit. Can we make a weapon out of anything, maybe something laying around?" Michael asked.

"No, I've already looked."

As Michael began to move, he noticed his back was in so much pain he could barely do anything. "How did you manage to get caught, Daniel? You had one job when you left the truck."

Daniel slumped his head.

"You came back for me, didn't you?" Michael asked.

"I heard the explosion. I thought you were dead..." Daniel mumbled.

Michael shook his head. "Dammit, Daniel."

Just then, a group of four guards barged through the door. They all held batons. The front guard barked something in English with a heavy Korean accent. He was taller than the others and appeared furious. His nostrils flared as he scowled at the Rangers.

"Who is...high rank? You?" The guard pointed his baton at Daniel.

"I'm in charge," Michael said without hesitation.

"You *were* in charge!" The man struck Michael over the head with the baton.

Daniel threw his body over Michael with his hands up. The other three guards joined in, beating both of them mercilessly. The prisoners groaned as each strike slammed into their bodies, but refused to give their attackers the satisfaction of crying out. Michael tried to fight back, but he was too weak.

He rolled over on his stomach as they continued to beat him, mouth pressed against the wet concrete and teeth clanging against it with every blow. He began coughing up blood. Then, without warning, they stopped.

Two of the guards picked up Michael under his arms, suspending him on the wall by a chain link harness. "You talk now... I tell you, you answer."

Michael could barely hold his head up. He watched blood from his head trickle down his left leg and drip on his bare middle toe. The guard dashed over and shoved his head up. "You hear me, American?"

"No habla Ingles." Michael grinned through bloody teeth. The head honcho punched his gut while two guards hoisted Daniel up, suspending him in an opposite chain harness.

"Now...you know where is base, American?" The Korean soldier pulled out a small map. Michael knew what he wanted. He wanted the locations of the American bases in South Korea.

"Name: Michael Keller, Rank: Staff Sergeant, Serial Number: 6783231498."

One of the soldiers whistled at the door, spewing off something in Korean.

A wheel squeaked. The noise got louder and louder. Then a large cage came into view. Inside were two massive animals obscured by a shadow.

The creature snarled as the cage was rolled into the room. All Michael could see was fur and fangs.

"I don't suppose that's dinner?" Daniel gave a raggedy laugh.

"You like?" Michael just gritted his teeth, too sore to even quip.

"Tell me *now* where is American base? You see, American? See how much bigger he is? Genetic engineered." He pointed at the black and grey monster in the dented steel cage.

The wolf drew his lips, exposing a pair of fangs about the size of a large man's ring finger. Saliva dripped from its mouth, smacking on the cage floor as it growled at a steady, low tone.

"Join the Army, they said. See the world, they said. Shit, Mike. I'm going to kick your ass if we die here!" Daniel pressed his back against the wall and huffed.

The Korean drew in a great breath. "We'll lower harness enough for wolf to snack on your feet and ankles. When finished, we bandage you. Then, if you don't tell me what I want, we lower a few more centimeters every day."

Michael gulped. "Daniel, we have to do this, man. Even if no one ever knows. Look at me," Michael said.

"Oh fuck no. Please God, why!?" Daniel cried out.

The guard smirked, pointing to his crotch. "The best part is when the wolf can reach here. He seems to enjoy that." "So, who's first?" The soldier licked his lips.

"I don't guess it really matters, does it?" Michael mumbled.

"As you wish. We'll let wolf decide then." He stood behind the cage and nodded at the guard by the door.

"Last chance," the guard said. He waited a couple of seconds then pulled the cage lever. The wolf shot out toward Michael, springing up before it latched on to his right ankle.

"Ahhhh-hhhhhh-hhhhh!" Michael yelled.

"You want to say anything, American?" The Korean glided up to Daniel while Michael was being mauled. Daniel shook but spoke only to Michael. "Mike?"

"No! D-Don't tell him shit!" Michael gasped. His eyes rolled back in his head as he went limp.

"This will be long week for both you." The guard snickered, strutting away.

***

Years before Michael stepped foot in North Korea, an explosion ignited earth's atmosphere. For almost two hours, night became day. Scientists and astronomers were baffled by the event. Everything from meteor showers, solar flares, and nuclear attacks were speculated then dismissed.

Then, the 'meteorites' came. Apparently, an object broke into several larger sections of debris before entering our atmosphere. During the descent, it splintered into thousands of smaller pieces. Fireballs crashed all over the globe, ranging from the size of a golf ball up to a small house. The death toll was relatively modest considering, with just under two hundred thousand casualties.

But that was just the beginning.

Even more shocking, the first reports indicated that the debris was wreckage from some type of craft. Some speculated it was a space station that had been shot down.

Based on the location and size of the explosion, experts calculated that the craft was nearly the size of four Empire state buildings. However, no satellites or sensors had detected the object before the explosion.

Government officials were reserved about using words that suggested the incident might have stemmed from something beyond our planet. However, hundreds of videos from people around the globe began flooding media sites, showing off strange materials from the wreckage. These objects had been forged into shapes, squares with exact angles or perfectly circular objects that did not occur in nature. Researchers confirmed through various rounds of testing that these objects did not come from our planet, shocking our civilization.

The proof was undeniable.

We were not alone.

Hundreds of top-level research companies halted their developments to focus solely on the acquisition of the alien meteorites, or *Star Rust*. It was an exciting time. However, underneath the enthusiasm, the gears of greed were already turning in the wrong direction.

The United States, North Korea, and China were the first governments to strike, recovering key pieces of the wreckage that propelled them forward militarily and economically.

Even in the short term, technological stepping-stones receded as companies leapfrogged into the future by reverse engineering the vessel's wreckage.

The U.S. secured an operational portion of the alien hull that used hypersensitive solar panels and cloaking technology. A powerhouse giant of a corporation was even rejuvenated from its discovery—SolarSystems. This juggernaut skyrocketed back to the top of the stock markets faster than any company in U.S. history.

They secured huge contracts with the Department of Defense, outfitting most vehicles with their solar technology. However, that wasn't enough. They wanted a piece of the war fighting as well. They invested in research and development of drone fighters that could take the place of elite soldiers. This didn't work quite as well. Artificial intelligence was fascinating on paper, but wasn't developed enough for execution in the field.

SolarSystems needed the human brain. They needed a Michael, but so did someone else...

Chapter Three

Seventeen weeks after Vala's transformation...

"Move it!" Vala hissed at a man running toward her with an awkward stride.

"I-I-I've been compromised," the young man said, catching his breath and looking back. Vala rolled her eyes. "Is *this* how it usually goes? My first time and you're late? Ugh, hand it over," Vala demanded.

He thumbed through his satchel. "Okay. Let me look... All right... There it is." He checked his left and right before carefully handing the object over to her.

She cupped it in her hands and her eyes lit up with wonder like a child holding a firefly for the first time. It was her first time seeing Star Rust. The small, angular alien object had an unusual blue-green shimmer unlike anything she'd ever seen. Some of it appeared scorched, but it was mostly intact.

"Well, it is pretty, isn't it? But not sure what all the fuss is about," she scoffed. Vala remembered a video she saw online. It featured a father heating a piece of the wreckage using a welder's torch, then quickly pressing the metal on his toddler's cheek. Most people gasped, thinking the child would be burned, but she wasn't.

"People die over Star Rust every day. Let's not add to the tally," He jerked his thumb over his shoulder. The shouting crept closer.

"Well, thanks to you, we're pressed for time," she replied, lowering her head and scowling at him, pushing some strands of hair out of her face.

He knew it was time to leave, but couldn't help noticing just how unnaturally beautiful she was. He'd heard the stories, but seeing a Cilan in person was unlike anything he could have imagined. It seemed a bit much though, as if something wasn't quite right with her. Her skin and hair looked *too* perfect, as though she were a walking, talking computer generated creation. Perhaps more seasoned Cilans could capture beauty without obvious perfection, but Vala wasn't quite there yet.

"You should have paid better attention on your way here." She peered around the corner. Her dog-like hearing could detect the police chatter blocks away.

"Well, we can't all be perfect, can we?" He shrugged it off, staring at her.

"Aren't you familiar with Cilans? Not exactly perfection with all these toxins running through my veins. I'm not doing this for the same reason as others."

He seemed intrigued by her comment. Cilans were typically ruthless, arrogant assassins. There were incidents of contractors like himself being murdered for being late.

"We all have our reasons. Listen, when the transfer is made, I'll put in a good word for you. But I'm curious about your, uh, specialty."

"Military focus," she replied immediately.

"Hmm, really? That's odd. Okay, assuming you get the job done, I might know someone... Call me when you're safe," he said, patting her shoulder.

"Later." She spun around with lightning speed and melted into the shadows.

The sirens blaring in the distance crept closer as she assessed her escape options. The city streets of Seoul, South Korea were littered with traffic at that hour, but not for long. Everyone was headed for cover.

The streets would be vacant soon because of the increasing radiation indexes. It was dangerous to stand out in this situation, but if someone hadn't fumbled the drop off point there wouldn't be a problem.

Vala glanced toward a bustling intersection. Nearly everyone was moving at a uniform pace. Many had their faces covered, pulling tight at their jacket collars or hoods while a light drizzle fell. She noticed a few tourists sprinkled about that looked a bit less accustomed to the flow of foot traffic. Their heads seemed to swivel around or peer up at the buildings and holographic billboards, contrasting the locals' dead ahead march.

Vala wasn't a native city dweller, but her new heightened sense of awareness made her feel more attentive. The controlled chaos around Vala offered her a sense of supremacy over the trotting cattle.

If it wasn't the unreliable liaisons or authorities, it was counter agents looking to steal her Star Rust. This first time, it was the local police. According to her VR modules, most agencies could only pick up traces of raw alien materials within a 20-mile range.

Luckily, even these new sensors weren't completely accurate. They could narrow down the location of the materials within a couple of blocks at best.

Vala crept toward a crossing, grabbing a comatose homeless person's shopping cart, she rested the object inside it. She draped a garment over the top to conceal her treasure. Pausing for a moment, she shook her head at what was in front of her. The owner of the cart was propped against the overpass support beam with a holovisor covering his eyes, ignoring everything around him. A stream of saliva ran down the corner of his mouth. His body jolted slightly as the cars on the bridge passed overhead.

He was young, early-thirties, and had a sophisticated, intelligent look about him. He could have been an attorney or banker. Now, he appeared forgotten. He was host to a parasite few recover from—technological addiction.

Ugghh, linkers.

She scoffed at him. She was disgusted by the disease. Her and Michael nursed his father back to health after a long, hard battle with it. He died a couple years later after the recovery from a heart attack, but he was himself at the end, not a slave to the addiction.

Suddenly, the thought was interrupted when a squad of police hoverbikes converged on the drop point like a swarm of hornets. These hoverbikes were crude, but visceral motorcycles that could hover in place and could match speeds up to 200 mph given a straight path.

Their powerful engines dispersed pools of water into mist, swirling it high into the air as people from the streets rubbernecked at the commotion. The squad was quite the intimidating spectacle of roaring engines and long, dark military-styled leather jackets that flapped in the wind.

The lead officer barked out a set of orders, pointing his men in all directions. One of the men beamed down on her position just as she darted into an alleyway.

Once in the alley, her hair changed to gray on the fly, and her skin aged forty years in less than a block. Her movements shuffled along naturally like an elderly woman.

The police fanned out in pursuit, splitting up as their sirens echoed off buildings and large holographic projector screens. One screen displayed a safety warning about wearing VR headsets and walking down the street. It depicted a short video of a young lady wearing a virtual visor then being struck by a car. A giant red X overlapped the screen on impact.

One of the officers caught a glimpse of the old woman shambling along. He hovered over her and shined his light directly on the Cilan, stopping her. He had to speak up over the bike's roaring engine. *"Ma'am!"* he demanded in Korean. She ignored him, looking straight ahead. He tilted his Hoverbike's vectored thrust exhaust, blowing her hood back.

Dammit. Can't an old woman be left alone?

She stealthily reached into her coat, gripping a compact version of the XMT 40 submachine gun. She flipped the safety off. Her body unleashed a surge of adrenaline four times that of a normal human, yet she appeared calm and harmless.

"Have you seen a young foreign man? He was in this area." The officer questioned her in a hurried tone. Vala had learned to speak some Korean from Michael, but her accent was off. To avoid risking suspicion, she mumbled off a slew of sounds that were unrecognizable in any language.

The officer immediately took his light away from her when he heard the senseless babble. He zoomed off into the distance, nearly clipping the side of the overpass before leveling out and darting into the neon night. She released her grip on the machine gun.

Vala let out a long sigh, leaning over the shopping cart. She surprised herself. He was simply a man doing his job. He could have easily had a family to provide for. She rubbed her eyes, putting her hands over her face for a moment. She recognized her readiness to kill was out of desperation.

She moved along at a snail's pace in crowded areas to avoid suspicion, but quickly shifted through dark alleys, gaining ground on her objective.

Vala passed by several linkers on her way. One group of four addicts were hooked together via virtual reality visors while leaning against an abandoned building. Another group of young people were taking hologram selfies with them, laughing at their demise.

She glared straight ahead, ignoring them. As she got closer, a young, stocky male took notice of Vala. "Hey, let's get a hologram with this old hag!" he shouted.

The man bounced over toward her, laughing. He started to put his arm around her, but when he did, she blasted him in the chest with the palm of her hand. The impact hurled him through the air and sent him tumbling end over end into a pile of trash.

The teens stopped laughing, staring motionless at Vala.

"Don't," she warned, stabbing her finger at the teens. They didn't say a word, backing away from the linkers as they scurried off into the streets.

She fled the scene, eventually approaching a dark, dingy pier on the Han River. A modest, unsuspecting fishing boat provided by her contractor awaited. Now, it was time for delivery.

***

Vala docked the boat at a pier deep in the North Korean wilderness. There was a dense mist smothering the morning sunlight. At the base of the pier stood two men, appearing as silhouettes. She moored the boat and slid around the back of the cabin while checking her submachine gun.

She tucked the Star Rust inside her coat and exited the boat, stomping toward the figures confidently. As she approached, she noticed the man out in front was of Asian descent, probably Korean, and the man slightly behind him was Caucasian. Both wore suits.

"You got it?" the Korean man asked.

"Maybe."

"Well, I hope you didn't come up here for nothing." He flashed a smile full of steel teeth.

"Right."

"So you don't want money, you want information?" he asked.

"Yes, I've made that clear, and supposedly your people can do this?"

"We find people that have the right tools for any job. People like yourself, for instance. People with information just require different sets of tools," he replied, sizing her up and down.

"Okay, so um, have you found Michael?" Vala asked.

"No, we haven't even started looking. You hand over the Star Rust, and we'll get you in contact with the right people." He spun around and huddled with his assistant.

Vala knew it was a risk, but she didn't have any better leads. She handed over the Star Rust.

"We'll be in touch, Cilan." He said.

In her mind, she had to believe Michael was out there somewhere.

And she was right.

Chapter Four

A middle-aged doctor shuffled down the hallway to welcome her new patient. Her glasses allowed her to see through special wall panels for each room, viewing each patient's vitals in an instant. A hologram of the doctor appeared in front of Michael.

"Hello, Michael. I'm your new physician, Doctor Haney. I'll be right down." The hologram flickered just before it disappeared.

"Okay. I'm not going anywhere," Michael mumbled.

This facility wasn't new; it had just been updated to accommodate modern technologies. From the outside, it had that early 2040's architectural feel. The style in that era was often overdone and exaggerated, and this one had too many angular lines for Michael's taste.

From a distance, it reminded him of an evolved version of a Roman cathedral. Designers wanted their signature mark on the most basic purpose structures, even if it looked horrid.

"Seem familiar? We're getting an unseasonably high amount of snow," the doctor said while entering the room. Michael was groggy, barely even acknowledging the doc's question.

"Welcome to Maine, Michael. I'm sure you'll be used to the snow and cold, being from Alaska." She smiled, gently cupping her hand along the contour of his partially deformed face. She glared down to where Michael's legs used to be.

"You'll be just fine," she whispered in a soothing tone. Michael detected her motherly attempt to comfort him.

"Dr. Haney, he's under contract, special orders from SolarSystems Corporation, he won't be staying long," the nurse whispered. The doctor quickly pulled her hand away as if it was next to an open flame.

"Oh. I heard a bit about him, but his chart is extremely vague. This is the one the Special Forces team found alive in that North Korean prison?" the doctor asked.

"Yeah, he was mumbling about it in his sleep. He and his cellmate had been mauled by some wild animal apparently. They just left his cellmate's corpse with him after he died."

"Oh my."

As Michael pried his eyes open, he noticed the nurse's hair as she scurried about. It reminded him of Vala's natural blonde color. He became intoxicated by the thought of her. He remembered the way her thick hair used to fall in front of her face when he pushed it behind her ears. The way her dimples only came out of hiding when she gave him a full smile.

"Well, hey there," the young nurse caught him looking at her. He quickly raised his eyebrows.

"Oh, no. Sorry. Something about you reminded me of um, someone," Michael said.

The nurse looked toward the floor and paused. "Oh? What was her name?" she said with a curious smile.

Michael turned his head away and answered softly. "Vala. Her name is Vala."

***

The next morning, Michael heard the heavy tap of army dress shoes approaching out in the hall. They had a certain sound that was recognizable, usually the stride exuded a confidence that only the most alpha Army guys had. He'd worn them a few times himself, but not as much as combat boots.

A serious-looking gentleman made his entrance into Michael's room in full US Army dress uniform, clutching his cap in his left arm. He was a husky man with a clean shave.

"Staff Sergeant Keller?" The man coughed. Michael noticed he was a staff sergeant as well, US Army.

"Hey…wait… Butch?" Michael whooped.

"Ha-ha! Took you a second without the beard, huh?" He grinned and tossed his big arms around Michael as he sat up in bed.

"Shit man, good to see you! You've gained weight? What are you, about two-sixty now?" Michael observed.

"Come on man, maybe two fifty. I don't know, gah, wow, good to see you too, brother! Been awhile." Butch said, patting Michael on the shoulder.

"How's Eve?" Michael asked.

"No idea honestly. I had to give my drone up when I got out." Butch replied.

"Oh. I thought you were still in?" Michael asked.

"No, I, uh, today I wore my uniform just to come see ya." Butch said.

"You didn't have to do all that." Michael said.

"Well...I wanted to. So, did they give you any cool hologram modules since you're lying around? I remember my uncle had this one when he was in the hospital. His was just sitting on a beach, they'd put a fan on him to simulate the breeze, seem to calm him—"

"Nope. I don't do holograms if I can help it. Bad experience." Michael interrupted.

"Yeah... *yeah*. Kinda makes me nauseated actually." Butch said, nodding his head slowly. Michael looked away. "Heard from any of the guys?"

"Not since I got out, after that last mission everyone sort of did their own thing, they put a lot of the guys into other units." Butch replied.

"Right, understandable. I'm sure you went to Daniel's funeral?" Michael raised his eyebrows. Butch sat down on the edge of the bed and turned his profile to Michael.

"Yep. Yours too." Butch dropped his head, stroking the top of his cap with his hand.

"How'd she look?" Michael asked, leaning to see Butch's reaction. He turned, staring intensely at Michael.

"Come on Mike. You know..." Butch said softly. His eyes watered up a bit as he looked away.

"...D-Did they at least let her sit up front, at the casket? We weren't married yet, so I worried about that." Michael asked as a tear rolled down his face. He clinched the bed sheets tightly.

"T-The row right behind that." Butch replied.

"Damn, well, not so bad I guess." Michael said.

"Yeah."

"Wait. How did you find out, you know, that I was—"

"Alive?" Butch interrupted.

"Yeah. She doesn't know, right? Everything's so hush hush." Michael asked intensely.

"Nope. Just me. Listen, Mike. Right after I got out, I applied to several different places. SolarSystems came calling." Butch said.

"Hmm. That's how you know. That's why you came in your uniform, they want *you* to confirm the contract with me. They wanted a familiar face for the homerun I guess."

"Yeah. My first day there they told me what you did, then asked me if I would do this. I couldn't pass it up man." Butch said grinning. "You don't know how good it is to see—"

"Oh, but I do! This actually works both ways," Michael said, pointing at Butch.

"Haha. I suppose so. I had to sign a non-disclosure form, the whole nine. I jumped at the chance to see you again though." Butch replied.

"They probably thought seeing you would make it easier." Michael said, shaking his head.

"Not so familiar though." Butch replied, running his hand across his shave.

"Yeah, now that you're out of the Army, you're clean shaven. Makes sense. I stayed on your ass for months," Michael said, raising an eyebrow.

"Haha."

"Vala get her check?" Michael asked.

"Not yet. After they get you over there, she'll get it." Butch said.

"Butch, man, you have—"

"I got it. Don't worry about that end of it. I'll make sure she gets it." Butch confirmed confidently.

"She needs that for treatment, man. I emailed the doctor's information to her best friend, her sister, and mother. I told them if anything ever happened to me to see that doctor. I know you understand and I appreciate you looking out." Michael said.

"No problem. Like I said, I got it." Butch said. Michael groaned up at the ceiling.

"Whew…good. So, any idea what will happen to me? What are they gonna do?" Michael asked.

"No. I don't know if I would tell you even if I did. I know it's not in my department though, it's some ultra-secret division, hush hush shit."

"Of course. Probably better if I don't know either." Michael said, raising his eyebrows. He noticed his hand shaking under the sheet. He quickly tucked it under his side to conceal it.

"Well, congrats on the job, Butch. Are they paying you good? You look well-fed of course," Michael grinned.

"Funny. Yeah about three times what I made as a Ranger, but with none of the risk other than the commute to work every morning," Butch said.

"What do they have you doing?" Michael asked.

"Desk jockey. I'm one of the liaisons for the Army, we're going after a few of their contracts, replacing post soldiers with drones. They do simple shit, standing guard for now."

"Hmm. I hope they're better than the drones we went up against in Korea." Michael replied.

"Those weren't bad actually, we were just good at taking them out." Butch said.

"If you say so... man I'm happy for you. Seems like a good gig. I think it'll work out fine." Michael said.

"Thanks. Listen, Mike... uhh. I don't, I really thought about all this before I came down here. Mike. I-I know who you are, as a man, I know how you think, putting others before yourself, many of them you didn't even know...I respect that, the guys respected that. I just wish that you valued yourself more, but really, I guess that's what makes you different. Much of it for me personally is selfishness. I don't want you to go away. I even tried to put myself in your shoes in this situation, and frankly, I'm not sure what I would do. I just—"

"Wait. You mean to tell me... if *Eve* needed a lifesaving procedure, you wouldn't risk your own skin? Unbelievable." Mike joked. Butch threw his hands up, smiling. "Guilty as charged. I like her and all, but she's not much of a cuddler, you know with blades on her hands and all? I like my smooth skin."

"Haha-ha...shit. Butch. I know...I just...Deep down for me maybe it's selfishness, too. Maybe I can't bear to see her in so much pain, maybe I don't want to see it, spiraling downhill. I just can't even begin to imagine that. Even then, what can I do? I can barely move myself. I can't even take care of her. Maybe this is my way of dealing with it. It's comforting to know she has another shot at life, and who knows, maybe she'll love again? That's what I keep telling myself anyway," Michael said. Butch tilted his head and cocked an eyebrow. He slowly shook his head.

"No talking you out of it?" Butch grinned.

"I thought you *liked* your new job?" Michael asked.

"I'm here for *you*, not them, especially when it comes to this," Butch said. Michael dropped his head, staring up at Butch.

"I figured as much. I've never seen you go back on what you want to do, but I thought I'd try. Well… let's see… here you go, sign and date this tablet, here and… here and you'll be off in no time," Butch said, gesturing at the tablet.

Michael signed without hesitation, handing it back to Butch. He stood up nodding his head, tugging his uniform down. "Always hated wearing these things."

"Bring it in one last time, you big ol' bear." Michael said. Butch gave him a hug. "I'll never forget who you are Mike…what you're doing for her now, and what you did for us out there. It's funny, you know when we got back, one of the guys, Mark? New guy, remember? Never said much?" Butch asked.

"Of course I remember. Short red head," Mike smiled.

"Yeah. Well his wife's pregnant." Butch said.

"That's…great! Wow. Well—"

"It's a boy. Yep. I heard uh, I heard they're naming it after you," Butch said, patting Michael on the shoulder.

"Whoa. That's special. I barely knew the guy." Michael said. He looked out the window, staring into the white horizon. Butch didn't say a word, he just let him absorb it for a moment.

"Yeah. Doesn't take long to figure what you're about. Okay. Do you, um, do you want me to keep quiet about all this, you know, maybe down the road I could tell Vala what you did here?" Butch asked.

"No. No. It'll be our secret. Listen. I really appreciate you coming to see me, Butch. It was great having you here," Michael said, staring at Butch intensely.

"Yeah, man. L-Least I could do." Butch nodded, his bottom lip quivered a bit as he looked over Michael one last time. Butch turned around slowly and exited the room.

Chapter Five

It had been seventy-two hours since Michael signed the final contract, and just as Butch promised, he was off to SolarSystems.

Waking up in a military helicopter was never a cheerful experience for Michael. In his army unit, if you woke up inside one, it meant you were heading to a bad place or had just left one. This time, he didn't even know where he was, strapped to a padded stretcher.

"Bravo six, this is Kilo seven. Package ETA in three minutes." The chopper pilot's lax voice was slightly muted by the rotor blades. The interior green lights reminded Michael of a war movie. Even though he had seen them plenty of times in real war, now they seemed different and foreign.

"Alright, Michael. Welcome to your new home," the pilot said over the intercom.

Michael couldn't see much from his position. A dense fog obscured the large, gray, boxy-looking installation with armed guards all around. The base was military style on the outside, large fortified gates with spotlights on every corner, but it had a corporate feel. Inside the walls it wasn't just soldiers, but mostly men in suits and doctors littered about.

SolarSystems started up after their acquisition of a key piece of alien Star Rust. They found hypersensitive solar receivers over 500 times more effective than those created with human technology.

Their reverse engineering of the materials found at the crash sites allowed them to dominate the stock market almost overnight. They landed huge contracts with Tesla, Ford, Honda, and of course, the Department of Defense.

SolarSystems equipped most of the military's equipment with this new solar-powered technology, allowing the United States to operate much more efficiently with almost no fuel costs. They aggressively protected the secret of the panel's technology, propelling the U.S. back into the superpower chair for a time.

Much of their mission was to sabotage competitors who were making progress in the field of solar technology. Profits did slump after this initial surge, so SolarSystems shifted their focus to experimental weapons prototyping.

As the chopper lowered, Michael could see a small group of medical staff waiting just outside the landing pad. They had their arms crossed low around their waistlines. They were a serious looking bunch. Their white coats flapped in the wind as the rotors swirled up dust at them.

After the chopper landed, a doctor in her late fifties entered. She was smirking and holding a syringe. Her hair was dyed dark and pulled back in a tight bun. She was pale and had a long face with chiseled features. She wore a long, light-blue lab coat with the SolarSystems insignia on it—a dark red sun with blue lettering through the middle.

"Hello, Michael. Welcome to SolarSystems," the doctor said. Her voice seemed as sterile and uninviting as the building itself as she navigated through the chopper toward him. He could smell her strong floral perfume before she closed the distance between them. The pilot coughed as she walked by.

She picked her way around the various cargo before getting within striking distance. Michael felt an overpowering sense of anxiety. He had no idea what would happen to him or if he'd ever wake up. He kept thinking about Vala and how much she needed him to do this. She'd never know what he went through, but it was all worth it.

Michael abruptly felt a hot jolt through his neck. He instantly slumped over.

"Hey, why'd you do that?" The chopper pilot leaned around and watched in confusion.

"They're easier to move around like this. I don't want him to see anything either. Any more questions, pilot?" the doctor said in a condescending tone. Michael began to black out from the shot but could clearly understand the chatter between the two.

"No, no more questions, *doctor*. Only a suggestion. You don't have to use the whole goddamn bottle of perfume. See that giant sixty-foot rotor blade above us? That's not an interior fan, as much as I wish it was right now." The pilot tipped an invisible hat.

Some of the lab workers outside the chopper attempted to hold back their laughter at the pilot's suggestion, while others completely lost it, doubling over and laughing hysterically.

The doctor didn't respond, but she was visibly perturbed by the pilot's smart-ass comment. She leaned out and turned toward two men holding their laughter, aggressively signaling them inside the chopper.

"Get him down to quarantine for a full cleaning! After that, send him to alpha processing. Now!" The doctor sternly ordered the men into action, pushing some loose strands of hair behind her ears that had fallen out of her bun.

The pilot's eyes followed Michael's body as he was transported right past her, she raised her eyebrows at him and slowly shook her head.

The intercom system announced a new delivery as Michael approached his initial cleaning and sterilization phase. "All stations. Be aware of delivery. All stations delivery." The message repeated a few times as Michael was pushed down the long hallway. His vision became spotty from the lights beaming down on him.

People that noticed Michael briefly stopped to examine his condition. Both his legs were missing below the upper thigh, along with some fingers on his left hand. He was also badly scarred from burns and puncture wounds.

Despite the sea of faceless onlookers, one man parted the waves to say hello. "Hey, guys. Hold up... Michael? Yeah, that's him. Hey, I'm Keith Sanders. I've heard a lot about you." The man stopped the workers transporting Michael.

He genuinely seemed concerned with a kind, reassuring voice. He patted Michael on the shoulder.

"Keith, we're on a tight schedule, can't this wait? You'll have plenty of time with him anyway—" The female doctor suggested.

"Did you actually welcome him here or are you treating him like a delivery? He's a human being." Keith growled.

"For now." The doctor mumbled. Keith stepped in close, eye to eye. "You treat him with respect, is that clear? We all know what he's sacrificed." Keith whispered, pointing at her sternly. She dipped her head away, then snapped back at Keith smirking. "Anything *else* Dr. Sanders?" She asked.

"No. Notify Dr. Amery he's here." Keith ordered, narrowing   his   eyes   at   her.

Chapter Six

A young secretary entered the room. "Dr. Amery, the package has arrived. Keith asked me to keep you updated."

Dr. Amery was already aware of it, so he briefly ignored her, jotting down a few notes regarding Michael. He stopped scribbling mid-sentence, losing his train of thought. "I *know,* Emily. Thank you." He faked a smile and nodded in approval. "That'll be all."

"Oh good." The secretary exited the room, slowly closing the door behind her. The sound of the door shutting still echoed throughout the great room. It was an office larger than a small house. Despite this fact, it was somewhat vacant, displaying only a few fishing photos. The walls were a midnight blue and the floors were carpeted in a lush green. An interior decorator he was not. He had a short game golfing setup that ran the length of the room and a few balls scattered about.

Amery took off his glasses and rubbed his eyes and face. "Ahhhhhh." His sigh was a blend of anxiety and moral conflict, an internal struggle on whether to abandon his ship or sail on.

Amery was calculating and decisive. He was average height, but with a stocky build. It was his Turkish heritage on mother's side to blame for that, he would always say. His hair was rather short and dark, but thick and wavy with a touch of gray spread evenly throughout. His skin was dark and leathered from summer fishing trips on the open ocean, and though he worked indoors, he yearned to be back outside.

Amery was once a competitive surgeon at Vanderbilt University in Nashville. Success fueled his drive so much that he took on too much work. Eventually, he lost his touch. A couple of malpractice lawsuits later, he decided to invest in a new startup company, SolarSystems, where he bought out majority ownership early on.

SolarSystems was already making strides in solar technology, but reverse engineered Star Rust propelled their research ahead at least three full decades. Now, Amery was considered the face of the corporate powerhouse.

Amery was poor growing up. His mother was a Turkish immigrant and his father was a subcontractor for a flooring company. His family traveled for work, living with relatives and friends throughout his childhood. Amery never had anything of his own when he was young. Often times, when his family would pick up and leave, his father would sell his personal belongings for travel expenses.

Amery would hide things to the best of his ability, but his father would usually end up finding them. One time, early in his high school years, Amery worked hard enough during summer jobs to afford an Hphone6, the latest holographic phone that was all the craze at the time.

He took hundreds of holographic photos, some of them very sentimental with his first girlfriend. However, his father found it and sold it for a down payment on construction equipment.

He lived in a total of twenty-two states, mostly out of RVs and trailers, during the first sixteen years of his life. However, Amery was an avid reader, and he studied voraciously, graduating early from high school with a full ride to Vanderbilt.

Needless to say, Amery enjoyed the finer things in life once he became an adult. He had things no one could take from him. Yachts, cars, and houses around the world. He had it all.

But Amery was a conflicted man. There was a part of him that cared about others. He wanted to see them healthy and happy.

However, a series of events unfolded that began to change him. Several years after becoming a practicing physician, Amery endured a horrible divorce. He lost nearly everything. Not just because of the divorce either. His ex-wife caught one of his houses on fire in a supposed accident, burning many sentimental items of Amery's.

Afterwards, greed overshadowed his consideration for others as he attempted to cling to his belongings. He didn't let people into his life anymore either. He began to look at patients as jobs rather than people. It was a slow process over the course of twenty plus years, but eventually, he was nothing like that ambitious med student who cared for others. Even worse, he was beginning to make irrational business decisions. Recently, he'd fired a seasoned department head over a simple disagreement.

"Emily, can you page Alpha to alert me when the package is ready?" Amery said. A pen dropped as her chair scooted away from the desk.

"Yes, Dr. Amery. I'll do it now," she shouted back through the open door.

Opening his top drawer, a small control pad automatically flipped out. He pressed a few buttons as a holographic display flickered while booting up. "Richard Amery," he commanded.

A voice activation responded back with a pleasant female voice. "Thank you, Doctor."

A screen showed various pictures of Michael Keller along with his medical history. Amery used his finger to glide through the various pictures. The first screen showed a brief summary of his official US Army final evaluation.

SSGT MICHAEL KELLER

US ARMY RANGER

SILVER STAR

PURPLE HEARTS (2)

TWO COMBAT TOURS

PRISONER OF WAR

SERVICE MEMBER COMMENTS: M. KELLER DISPLAYS A COMBINATION OF INNOVATION, RESOLVE, AND LEADERSHIP THAT EXCEEDS US ARMY RANGER STANDARDS. HIGHLY RECOMMENDED FOR RETENTION. COLONEL RONALD OLIVER, US ARMY.

Amery cycled through several pictures of Michael and his unit. Most were poses of the men in training. Amery's staff had even dug up a few files of his civilian life too. They had found photos of Michael and Vala. It appeared that he was on leave during most of the pictures. They were smiling in every photo together, embracing each other and glowing with happiness.

"Hmm, tragic... So young and happy..." He examined the photos with a jeweler's eye.

The next display showed a brief outline of the incidents involving Michael while in the service. One was a grisly scene depicting him after his return to allied forces. He was a POW in North Korea, captured after his unit disarmed a nuclear weapon.

According to the official military report, Michael and his fellow Ranger Daniel Naben were rescued by US Delta Force, but Naben died due to his injuries.

Amery shifted the hologram and drew up a 3D diagram of medical operating procedures. It showed insertion points of various cybernetic implants and gave options for each, considering Michael's specific injuries.

Suddenly, there was a knock at the door. "Richard."

"Yes, come in," Amery said, recognizing the voice. A shadowy figure entered the room. He was a tall and lanky man, dressed in a dark, slightly oversized suit. He strutted in as Amery stared at him.

"You're gonna love this, you really are..." The man smirked.

"What? I don't have time for games. Any new Star Rust leads? Intelligence?" Amery asked.

"Both," the man said as he plopped down in a chair in front of Amery's desk. "Done any golfing lately?"

"Just spill it, you know we've lost a lot of field assets lately. I need Star Rust. Not in the mood." Amery demanded.

"Ahhh, all right damn. You're getting crankier the older you get. Okay... so your, ah, Vala Thomas, the girl we've been following?"

"Yes..."

"Well, after she deposited her payout, she immediately went to Germany."

"For vacation? I don't care what she does with the money."

"No, no... This bitch...*she's* running Star Rust contracts as we speak. She went to Germany to undergo Cilan therapy," the man said. Amery stood up, pushing his glasses forward and putting his hands out on the desk in front of him.

"I want you to understand this is not a joking matter. It's not funny." Amery asked sternly, but softly. He looked a thousand miles away.

"Kinda sounds like that, but no, no I'm not. She went off the radar when she went to Germany, then she popped up again, but she looked much different. We did some digging and turns out she's been asking all over the place about a man named Michael Keller. She's willing to do contracts for any information on his disappearance," the man said.

"This isn't happening." Amery bit his lip.

"Oh, so that's your boy? This…Michael Keller? The one we have here?" the man said, looking at a holographic display. Beside the human figure was another, one that appeared humanoid, but much more sinister.

"You're gonna turn him into *that*?"

"Yes…DAMN!" Amery exploded, smashing his fist into the desk violently. A golf ball popped up out of a cup holder and rolled off the desk toward the man. He picked it up and placed it back in the cup. Amery's face was red, boiling with anger.

"You want me to deal with her?" the man asked.

Amery paused for a moment before pacing the length of the room. The man waited patiently.

"How many times have you tried to *deal* with a Cilan?" Amery asked.

"Uhhhh—"

"Exactly. You'll be killed. She'll kill you and your goons. Listen. I want you to find a way to lead her to me, anonymous and all that shit...as if I'm a contact point for information about Michael, an insider. Make it seem like I can find him," Amery said.

"Kinda risky, but that should be easy enough. Then what? Is there something in it for you, she'll be skeptical otherwise?" he asked.

"I've lost most of my Star Rust trackers this year, until we find some replacements... I have an idea. Two birds with one stone. Vala is going to do a lot of work for us...for free. When people do things for money, sure, they get things done, but when they do things out of desperation—well, they can move mountains. If she wants to play private investigator, then she'll build us a mountain of Star Rust. I'll keep her busy away from other sources. *Then*, we can deal with her, that'll give us time to figure out how," Amery said.

"Damn." The man shook his head, smirking as he stood up. He grabbed a golf putter leaning against the wall and lined up a shot. He took it, narrowly missing. "Ahhh, almost..." he said.

He whistled at Amery as he ducked through the door. "Remind me never to piss you off."

"Shut the door!" Amery hollered. "Always leaves the damn   door   open."

Chapter Seven

Two weeks later...

"Keller." A man said as Michael woke up.

"Y-Yea?" Michael said blinking his eyes. He was heavily sedated.

"I saw you looking under your sheets at your new legs. Amazing, aren't they?" He asked.

"I thought it was a dream, they're metal, or something, why do I have eagle talons for toes...who, who are you?"

"Dr. Amery. I'm the guy that gave you those legs. You're fine. You did well in surgery."

"I can walk again?" Michael asked. Dr. Amery looked over his vitals on a small holographic display beside his bed.

"You will, you'll run too... you know, organic-like movements were probably the most difficult aspects of creating machines in the beginning. As you can see, it's so advanced now, they exceed even biological life forms."

Michael glared at Amery, then back down at his new legs. "I've seen something like them...in a movie," he mumbled.

"Probably not like those." Amery pushed his glasses forward. "Michael, it's very possible you'll be able to reach over 60 miles per hour in short bursts."

Dr. Keith Sanders knocked on the door. "You've met Keith?" Amery glanced up.

"I-I don't know. Wait. Yeah. I was a bit out of it, but I remember," Michael said, leaning his head up slowly.

Michael took a deep breath. "Has she received her payment?" Michael asked, lowering his voice.

"Yep, a few days ago," Amery said confidently. "I thought you might ask. You put in your contract that you'd want to see this...and your Army buddy, Butch... Yeah, he's a good friend, isn't he? He won't stop asking either. Thing is, I'm not sure you'll remember any of this anyway."

"I-I want to see. It'll put me at ease. I just, I can't take care of her like this. I needed to find a way," Michael insisted, zoning in and out.

"Yes, Michael. I know. You did everything you could, and I admire a man like that." Amery said. Then, he pulled out a tablet that detailed the contract's transaction. "As you can see here, your Vala had booked a vacation. Looks like Germany. Ah, Munich, actually," Amery said, smiling. Keith cut his eyes over at Michael, his head slumped low with his hand under his chin.

Amery cycled through a slide of bank transactions with a photo of her at a local bank. "See, there she is just before the transaction, and now she's been paid in full," Amery said, showing Michael her bank account with over 3.5 million dollars. Michael's face abruptly changed to panic when he saw her. It was a small surveillance photo of her inside a bank, but it was enough.

Michael grabbed Amery's lab coat. "Whoa... Hey, Michael, um..."

Michael fought off his hyperventilation. Seeing the look on Vala's face felt like a burning coal inside his chest. He'd never seen such sadness in her eyes. In that moment, he realized what he'd done was a mistake.

"Noo-oo! I shouldn't have. I-I've made it worse...I should just be with her, even like this. No! Please. She needs me! Can I please go to her? I don't want this!" Michael said, holding his chest. His body shook. His face turned red as he pulled down on Amery's coat, tearing it.

"Whoa. Whoa. Keith?! A little help here," Amery said.

"Michael," Keith said softly, putting his hand on Michael's shoulder.

"Let me see her. You have to let me see her..." Michael demanded.

"Now, Michael, calm down. What—" Amery started.

"Now!" Michael tried to pull Amery towards him, but claws in his talons ejected outward, shredding the bed sheets.

Keith darted over to the nurse's station, grabbing a syringe.

"Please! We'll pay it back. We'll give all the money back! I have to get back to her! Please help me! I-I've made a mistake here," Michael pleaded desperately. His hands began to shake before he felt a hot jolt in his neck, loosening his grip on Amery.

Keith clenched his arm, injecting a sedative into him. "It's all right, Michael." Michael almost immediately passed out.

"Ahhh, didn't expect that honestly." Amery said.

"You show a man the love of his life when he *knows* he can't have her again. What the hell is wrong with you?" Keith raised his voice, pulling his hair back while pacing the room.

"He put it in his contract, Keith. He specifically wanted to see her after the money was deposited. I told him after we had him here we would—"

"After you had him at the point of no return *then* you would show him. How honorable, you kept your word," Keith said, shaking his head.

"Well, I needed to make sure he wasn't going to back out. I need him here first. I just—didn't expect *this* reaction. I thought he knew what he wanted here. I had him sedated enough where I thought he'd stay calm," Amery said, staring at the floor.

"What reaction *did* you expect?" Keith demanded.

"I thought this was a win for all three parties. I'm not sure what he expected to see, of course she wouldn't look happy," Amery said.

"Well, good luck in your next round of surgery now. You lay someone down in this state of mind and you already know the possibilities..." Keith said.

"You let *me* worry about that," Amery replied, walking out of the room.

SolarSystems had always had the human option in their back pocket. They had researched and tested artificial intelligence, but it just couldn't match the millions of years of evolution the human mind had undergone. However, this emotion, this attachment, was the price for all the dynamic intelligence the human brain offered.

***

"Dr. Amery, you have a call from one of your field assets. Should I take a message?" a young secretary questioned.

"No, no. Put them through."

Amery hesitated before picking up the phone, tapping his fingers on the desk. He was in deep thought. He had plenty of field assets acquiring Star Rust, and most of them called from unregistered numbers, but there was one in particular he didn't want to hear from. Not after what happened with Michael.

"Um, yes," he answered politely. He gulped.

"Are you going to tell me your name at some point?" Vala asked.

"I don't do that. I have anonymous sources too, you know, and I never ask them that question," Amery replied.

"Whatever. Well?" she asked.

"You'll be happy to hear I have a name for you. Someone who's involved," Amery said.

"Let's hear it," she said.

"Lucas Anderson," Amery replied.

"I've never heard that name before. Anything else?" she asked.

"Nope, that's it. I would wager in your line of work that's all you need is a name. I hope you find what you're looking for," Amery said. Vala hung up the phone immediately.

"If she only knew Michael was less than sixty feet away from me. Hm. She would likely kill everyone in this building to get to him, even me." Amery said raising his eyebrows. He leaned back in his chair, interlocking his fingers as he stared at the wall.

After surgery, Michael would begin training with Keith Sanders. Then, all the cumulative research and drilling would be put to the ultimate test. SolarSystems would have to prove their newest iteration to the Department of Defense if they wanted to land a huge contract.

In order to do so, SolarSystems would need to pass *The Crucible*—a military war game designed to test the very best.

It was created specifically to measure the ability of new military prototypes to outwit the human mind. However, after years of failure, SolarSystems discovered the only way   to   fight   fire   was   with   fire.

Chapter Eight

Eight months later at The Crucible...

At a remote military facility in Alaska, two men stood silently for a moment, looking over the balcony and collecting their thoughts. They stared into the white woodlands as the snow fell. They had just arrived, and it was a rare moment of beauty, as both men were used to the decaying mainland United States.

"You know, other than the radiation levels, it almost appears untouched," Lucas said.

"Until you realize you've grown an extra toe or finger from the exposure," Keith replied.

Keith Sanders was the behavioral expert in charge of SolarSystems' newest prototype. Keith was Dr. Amery's right-hand man. This wasn't his first rodeo. He had seen a few iterations of new weapons programs come through the pipeline at SolarSystems, but this new model was much different.

Keith had spent the last eight months instructing his newest prototype, the former Army Ranger Michael Keller, on the training grounds at SolarSystems. However, this facility in Alaska would be the final assessment before he could be considered an active military unit, giving SolarSystems the chance to score a massive military contract. The Crucible was about to get underway.

Keith was a thirty-eight-year-old man from Minnesota, but didn't have the accent. Most of his family were devoted

Roman Catholics, but Keith labeled himself simply as a "believer" without a denomination. He'd been at odds with his family for years over his faith, especially his father who saw Keith as the black sheep. Despite his success in school and his career as a behavioral scientist, his father never really got over his faith choice.

Up until a few years ago, Keith sported thick blond hair and a white smile. Nearly wrinkle-free skin made him look ten years younger than he was. He attributed it to his vegan diet. However, he'd begun to age quickly in the last few years. His hair had thinned and developed a bald spot on the top back portion of his head, and many of his wrinkles looked more pronounced.

He was less than an inch short of being six foot tall, but unlike most, he didn't round up. He usually dressed well, but here in the frigid cold, he wore a dark, heavy pea coat with a black scarf.

He ate right, worked out, and didn't smoke or drink much. Most of his focus on health was a distraction for the past. Being health conscious was time consuming, and along with his work, that's exactly what he needed.

Tragically, Keith lost his newborn son and wife in a surprise radiation storm and law restricted access to hospitals or any government buildings during these events. His wife went into labor early from the stress of the storm, and bled to death.

Over the last year, he'd moved his focus in life into other areas, specifically work. He forced himself to become a busy man.

"What do you have planned after the Crucible?" Lucas asked.

"Nothing really. This is all I've been planning for months."

"What about you? Headed back over to Fifth Column after all this is over, or do you have business elsewhere?" Keith asked.

"Oh yeah, a lot of work waiting for me. It never ends. I'm hoping the materials we tracked down help your new prototype ace this final test." Lucas answered, tugging his coat tighter around his chest.

"*Our* prototype, you mean," Keith corrected, smiling.

"Well, yes, of course."

Keith and Lucas weren't exactly friends, but they knew each other through Dr. Amery. Amery was gifted at finding the right people for the right role, and Lucas could find anything. He was a hunter of Star Rust.

Lucas Anderson was a legend in the eyes of many. He was a former Navy SEAL commander in the North Korean campaign, and now was leader of the ultra-secret *Fifth Column*, one of SolarSystems' business partners. He was there to see just how much his expeditions had contributed. A contract extension was at stake.

Lucas' official title was CEO of the Fifth Column. His real title was *external acquisitions*. Basically, his company was responsible for acquiring alien Star Rust by any means necessary. It was a very specialized trade, and Lucas' company was just right for the job. He had assembled a mega cast of the best mercenaries, intelligence specialists, engineers, and logistics experts in the world, most of which were connections he made while in the SEALs.

However, under the table, SolarSystems was looking to cut out Lucas' company. Lucas and his men had acquired some of the materials for this prototype, but ironically, it might put them out of the job. One of the prototype's design objectives was to hunt down additional Star Rust.

"Whoa, that wind just cuts right through you, huh?" Lucas said.

"Eh, I'm kinda used to it. Not quite this cold though," Keith said.

"Where you from again? Like, Oregon, wasn't it?"

"Ha, Minnesota," Keith answered.

"Ah yeah. I knew it was one of those places where you guys brag about your driving skills in the snow." Lucas grinned. "Or how you don't need coats, just grow a beard and chest hair and you'll be fine."

"I've never heard a man from Minnesota say that." Keith said.

"Who said it was a man?" Lucas posed.

"And I thought the Marines were the jokesters." Keith smiled.

"That's why you left, is it?" Lucas joked. "Nothing wrong with a little body hair here and there."

"To each his own I suppose."

Lucas hummed as he came inside, patting Keith on the back. Keith stayed out on the balcony for a few more minutes, taking it all in. He looked out at the scenic snowscape that blanketed the woodlands as the winds howled through the abandoned military structure, pushing drifts of snow up twenty feet high around the concrete perimeter walls.

Immediately down from the installation, he could hear the warped metallic hangers from an old electric tower creaking in the wind. The electric lines still dangled in the snow like loose strings.

The area had suffered minimal fallout during the North Korean attacks years ago, but the readings were supposedly "safe" for military personnel. Civilians never reoccupied.

Keith went back inside. "Say, Lucas. How many Marines are participating?"

"Twenty-two, I think," Lucas replied, counting in his head.

"You'll be surprised when you see our work. It's nothing like what we've had in the past," Keith said.

"Well, I just hope we've assisted enough in the development. We weren't allowed to see much of it at all, even in the early stages. I barely even saw what we recovered," Lucas said, pulling out a tablet.

"Like you would have any idea what it is anyway." Keith said.

"What?" Lucas squared up on Keith, grinning.

"You don't know what you're looking at, you just have the right people working under you."

"And what's wrong with that?" Lucas asked.

"Nothing, I just like giving you a hard time. I do think it's humorous how much work you do in the field, yet you probably don't know what any of it does."

"But I can find it. I can get my guys close enough, that's more than half the battle in my field. I know my role." Lucas explained.

"Right."

"Well it looks like *your* men are moving quickly. They're almost set up for the drill," Lucas noted.

Keith looked outside, and to his surprise, most of his men were finished ahead of schedule. They were underdressed.

"It's amazing how fast people will work to get out of the cold," Keith said, smiling. "Three of my guys are brand new. I told them to dress warm but—"

"Must be Minnesotans?" Lucas said.

"Ha, yeah." Keith chuckled and thought about the freezing temperatures Lucas probably endured during SEAL training. SEALs were known to spend most of their time in and out of hypothermic conditions. Keith didn't have a clue what real cold was and he knew it. Minnesota-born or not.

"All the solar generators are up and going. We'll use the old guard stations for observation. The rest of the facility will have power by the time the Marines arrive," Keith said, looking out into the snowstorm.

"How much solar power are you getting through those thick clouds?" Lucas asked.

"Enough. It's a good thing we don't have the old solar receivers. Those wouldn't have picked up anything from this. It's no wonder they never restored this place."

"Not sure I blame them." Lucas grinned.

"Me either. Oh wait... Do you hear that? I think our Marines are already here." Keith and Lucas looked up toward the horizon. It was difficult to see, but a dark mass faintly crept closer.

"Oh, wow. They're here early," Keith said.

Suddenly, the U.S. Marine Wraith transport jet approached, doing a flyby of the installation before circling back around. The pressure from its vertical thrusters twirled up snow, casting it into the distance.

Keith could hear the Marines' chatter on his audio sensor as they landed. "Well, this is it," the pilot mumbled under his breath while looking across the abandoned arctic military installation. "Ain't much to look at," he said in a southern accent.

It was a large, dull-looking complex. From the air, one side was stacked with metallic, igloo-like storage bins. The other side had a massive hanger bay on the south corner that connected to a bank of office buildings. A few abandoned tanks, jeeps, and helicopters littered the white airstrip. The air control tower was at the north corner. Its glass had been blown out long ago and it was now filled with snow.

As unimpressive as it appeared now, it was once one of the largest active military bases in North America, complete with an underground facility.

A holographic visor automatically flipped down in front of the pilot's vision, assisting with the landing in the heavy snow. The rest of the Marines were sleeping in the back compartment, swaying back and forth in their harnesses as the storm's turbulence nudged the jet around slightly.

"Alright, people. Naptime is *over*! Get your gear and muster with Staff Sergeant Garza," the captain yelled out. Even though he raised his voice, he was completely calm.

Keith looked out the main deck's window, wiping away the steam from his breath on the glass. The Marines filed into the courtyard in front of them. They were an impressive and intimidating bunch. Despite being groggy from their naps, their weapons looked as if they could level the entire compound.

"*Attention on deck*!" Garza shouted, but her voice was lost in the blizzard.

"It's cold, Staff Sergeant. I can't feel my face," one of the corporals joked from the middle of the ranks.

Garza marched between the ranks, moving the Marines aside as she pushed toward the outspoken Marine. "You won't ever be able to feel your face again if you have another outburst like that. You're a Marine. Shut your damn mouth and await further instructions—all of y'all," Garza ordered as a few of the Marines chuckled.

Finally, the captain appeared, ducking under the door from the transport jet. He counted his men by hand as he approached them.

"All right. The head count is twenty-two. That's everybody. Get 'em inside, then we'll muster back out here at 0700." Like the corporal, he seemed to have had enough of the cold.

Captain Marcus Belmont was of superhero stature. He played football for the Naval Academy as a defensive lineman. He was six foot nine inches and over 300 pounds. He set the record for deadlifting 1,130 pounds while he was still at the academy. His temperament was measured, but he had a short fuse.

He had intelligence to boot, graduating third in his class at the Naval Academy. He spoke with an urban southern accent that some pinned as uneducated, but they couldn't have been more mistaken.

Belmont grew up in New Orleans after oceans had swallowed the downtown district with rising sea levels. Most people fished Bourbon Street afterwards, but that eventually went away too as the demand outweighed the supply.

Belmont strolled inside the main deck where Lucas and Keith were. He ducked under the doorframe as one of Keith's crewmen watched on. "Shouldn't he be in the NFL?" Lucas joked, leaning in toward Keith. Belmont stepped toward them confidently, almost hurried.

Keith raised his eyebrows and nodded his head, acknowledging the comment. He had known Belmont from a previous Crucible. They weren't friends, but they weren't enemies. The interaction was always the same—Belmont's unit would show up, trash Keith's prototypes, then leave.

However, Belmont had apparently never met Lucas. Keith remembered his manners, glancing toward Lucas. "Oh, Captain, good to see you. This is—"

"Lucas Anderson, Commander of Seal Team Six, Star Rust mercenary. He don't need no introduction," Belmont interrupted, smirking.

"The man does his homework...or he watches a lot of TV." Lucas grinned and nodded while shaking his hand and looking right into his eyes.

"Lil' bit of both, really," Belmont replied.

Lucas had a rough but calming look you didn't forget, like the modern Marlboro man with a few more scars and tattoos. He wore a dark suit with an overcoat. His crisp, modern style tossed a coat of civilized paint over him that didn't quite cover the dirty walls underneath. He was mysterious but approachable.

All his dealings with alien artifacts made one wonder exactly what he'd seen, and that being a former Navy SEAL commander anchored down his tough guy credentials. Not that he cared.

His eyes seemed even bluer in person than in the TV news interviews he was a regular on, always answering questions about his organization. His tanned skin contrasted the white, wavy hair that flowed around his head. It curled up the back and around his ears, appearing wild, yet well maintained.

He wouldn't have gotten nearly as much attention if not for his looks and mysterious aura, but public opinion of both SolarSystems and the Fifth Column was at its best when Lucas was on TV. However, he'd recently moved back to the ground level of his work after his contract extension was at stake. Normally, he would never even be out there.

"Ah, okay, right. Well, you remember me? I'm Keith Sanders, the prototype's behavior and training supervisor." Keith stuck out his hand to shake, noticing Belmont's hand was easily double the size of his own. Belmont shook hands and gave Keith a sample of his power, enough that it wasn't too obvious.

"Okay, so how many of these things are my men going against this time?" Belmont questioned, looking out the window with arms crossed.

"Ah. Umm…well, sir. There's only one prototype this time," Keith said.

"*Haha!* One? Hold on. Did—you—just—say…*one*?" Belmont snapped around with a big smile.

"That's it," Keith said, smiling back and crossing his arms.

"You mean to tell me, you had all this set up for *one* prototype to fail? I denied four of my men's leave requests to haul them here…for this? You do know that drones and prototypes are our *specialty,* right? You had three of them last year, and how did that work out for you?" Belmont turned his back to them, shaking his head.

"Not well," Keith acknowledged. He dipped his head with his hands crossed out in front of him.

"Exactly… Pshhh, we might as well go ahead and leave now," Belmont said confidently.

Lucas was silent during the conversation. He simply grinned politely, glancing back at Keith.

"Ridiculous," Belmont went on. "Fine, we'll be up at 0700 and you or whoever can debrief my men on the situation. *You* can explain why they're up here freezing for a single prototype's testing," Belmont said, leaving the room and snickering. "Whole lotta trouble for nothing, man."

As Belmont exited the room, Keith and Lucas looked at one another. Keith shrugged, shaking his head. "I'm not explaining anything to his men. I'll let my prototype do the talking," he said in a confident tone.

Belmont's unit was in fact an elite Marine unit, a Special Forces division designed to deal with threats such as advanced drones with or without artificial intelligence. They were equipped with weapons and tech that focused on disrupting sensors and electronic systems most drones needed to function. They were proven in real combat from the North Korean campaign, not just drills and war games like the Crucible.

"He seemed thrilled," Lucas said sarcastically.

"That's the happiest you'll see him." Keith twirled around, lasering Lucas with his eyes. "There's a reason we're only testing one prototype against his whole unit."

"Because you enjoy losing?" Lucas smirked.

"Ha, I'll show you," Keith said.

"Sure. I'm interested in seeing it, but one question," Lucas posed.

"Shoot."

"I heard the last Crucible against these Marines was really...*short*? How long did your three drones last out here?" Lucas asked, raising his eyebrow.

Keith sighed and paused briefly, hoping Lucas' interest in the question would fade, but it didn't.

"Ahhh, well, once the drill commenced, about twenty minutes," Keith said, lowering his voice when he said the number.

"Hmm, well, don't feel bad. Professional fights last only a few seconds sometimes," Lucas said with a serious face.

"True, but they don't have to cover five square miles in their ring. Most of that time was travel time." Keith grimaced.

"Ouch. Then, yeah, that's really fast I guess... Hey, I tried." Lucas patted Keith on the back.

"Nice try." Keith laughed.

***

Belmont and his Marines settled into their bunks for the evening. Belmont patrolled the compartment, assessing his men's level of confidence and morale.

"You good?" he asked one of his men.

"Yes, sir." The young man nodded, sitting on the edge of his bunk. He seemed a bit nervous about it all. He'd never participated in these games.

Belmont sat down on the bunk opposite him. Looking across, he paused for a moment, rubbing his hands together. "Look, tomorrow, we don't need any doubt going into this.

None. We've never lost one of these games." He crossed his arms at the young Marine.

"I understand, sir." The boy squared his shoulders, but kept shuffling his feet around.

"The reason we've never lost is because no one has a face like I'm looking at now. Better perk up, Marine. Did you break up with your girl or what?" Belmont snorted, trying to keep too much condescension out of his voice.

"No, sir."

"What is it then? You, *concerned*?" Belmont asked, leaning in.

"Sir, I'm just nervous. I have anxiety and—"

Belmont interrupted him. "All right, look. Go relieve the security patrol from Corporal Stewart. You're like a black hole of pity sitting here in the middle of everyone, sucking the life out of my entire unit... Go!" The Marine snapped up quickly, grabbing his gear and running out of the compartment.

Belmont had his own way of doing things, and regardless of opinions about his style, he produced results. With his temper, he had less chance of making the rank of Major unless he could win.

Part of the problem with making rank was that he pushed things a bit too far, even having been accused of physically assaulting his men. Nothing had ever been proven, but there was enough evidence from different situations to suggest a problem. Only one of the Marines currently serving with Belmont had testified against him. The other two were transferred.

Chapter Nine

Later that evening, Keith took Lucas down to the storage area where he stashed his new prototype. Lucas was completely unaware of what he was about to see. His company had only contributed to about 15% of its development and all of that was just recovering the alien materials. He had no idea what they used them for.

The journey down to the basement was eerily quiet. People had used that tunnel to evacuate during the fallout warnings back in the war with North Korea. Being a military base, soldiers and their families herded through these tunnels to safety, but some people didn't make it. The story said that the installation's commanding officer tried to force some of the civilians out of the shelter. Claiming he needed to conserve his combat strength. Needless to say, that didn't work out so well.

The Army didn't like the term mutiny, but the ensuing "riot" left the base commander, plus hundreds of troops and bystanders, dead without a single radiation casualty. Since they were in a war zone though, the incident was swept under the rug. The dead simply tagged "Killed in Action."

"So, you taking me down to the dungeon?" Lucas joked.

"Yeah, fitting term down here," Keith said.

"I heard about it too, the riot, but don't know the details," Lucas said.

"Me either. I just know a lot of people died down here. Crazy the things that happened during the war most never knew about. Mutiny is a fascinating dynamic, especially in an area this desolate. Might as well be on the open sea," Keith said.

"I'm sure they had to stay down here with the radiation levels above. Must have been hell cramped in here," Lucas examined.

"Claustrophobia and enochlophobia sufferers would have had it the worst."

"*Eno-chlo-what?*" Lucas said.

"Fear of crowds. This place must have been shoulder to shoulder."

"Yeah, really. With the size of the base, I doubt everyone could fit," Lucas replied. "But I know I'd rather be inside during a radiation event than outside. At least I can fight back against people. Out there, you have no chance."

Keith didn't say anything. Lucas' comment brought back a memory he'd rather shut out completely. "All right, just around the bend here. Can't wait for you to see it," Keith said, peering around the corner. He fought back a horrible thought about his wife's last moments. He pulled ahead a few paces so Lucas couldn't get a read on his emotional state.

"Great place to store the prototype. Unsuspecting, for sure. Doubt anyone would think to come here," Lucas said.

"Yeah, well, I had to put the prototype somewhere none of those Marines could find him. Not that they would do anything, but some of the younger guys might get bored."

As they navigated down the hall, an odor began to surface, like old, damp carpet inside an abandoned house. Keith toggled a green light on his tablet. It illuminated part of the corridor. Some of the passage lights flickered, creating a slow strobe effect. Rats scurried about, darting in and out of holes and between their feet.

"Whoa, lots of rats!" Keith picked up his foot and let a few run underneath him.

"Your prototype's first test tomorrow: survive the rat-infested dungeon." Lucas smirked.

"Ha, well that might be a test for us. I'll give the prototype orders to exit out of the fallout shelter away from the base. When he comes back topside, that'll put him at the starting location for the drill," Keith said, stepping over some old clothes piled in the hall.

"Whoa..." Lucas said, checking under his foot.

"What?" Keith asked.

"There are a few skulls in that pile of clothes over there."

"Damn!" Keith panned his light over it. They both froze.

The skulls were arranged side by side, facing outward in the same direction. One of them had a blunt force trauma wound, cracking the skull, while the other two looked like execution-style gunshot wounds.

"Those were prisoners, someone's prisoners..." Lucas said. "Two males and looks like a... young female maybe?" Lucas inspected the skull a bit closer. He appeared extremely calm, meanwhile Keith's hands were shaking as he held the light.

"You okay over there?" Lucas glanced back at him.

"Yeah. All right, yeah. Let's move on. The rats are enough to deal with down here. We're almost there, just around this bend here," Keith explained.

"Lead the way," Lucas said.

"I don't particularly like dead things," Keith replied.

"It's the things that are alive that will hurt you," Lucas added.

"Physically, maybe," Keith said.

Suddenly, Keith's tablet illuminated an upright stasis pod. It was a large metal cylinder with a glass panel on the front.

Lucas stopped several feet away. Keith went on ahead of him, wiping away the moisture on the glass with his hand. His green tablet light gave way to a frightening image—a metallic, human-like skull inside. Lucas immediately reacted, taking a quick step back as if he was startled.

"Ohhh, my... *What* is that?" Lucas asked, putting his hand under his chin. It appeared as if a team of psychologists specializing in nightmares put together the most terrifying imagery they could for the face. A metallic monster that shared similarities with a man.

"Why does the skull resemble a human?" Lucas asked, probing in closer.

"Well..."

"It's human, isn't it?" Lucas said confidently.

"Partly. Only certain elements remain. I'll explain," Keith said.

"If the public ever finds out you've used a person for this..." Lucas said, shaking his head.

"We," Keith corrected.

"We?" Lucas stared at Keith, confused.

"We, Lucas. Your company is labeled as a partner with the design of this unit," Keith said, grinning. "I suggest you keep all of this to yourself."

"I never knew about any of this, Keith, and you know it."

"I understand that, but neither did the security guard that let me in the gate at SolarSystems every morning, but you know what? We're all involved. I had no idea what we were doing in the beginning either. It's all Dr. Amery. I just work for him."

"You're a behavioral expert and psychology guy. You thought you'd always be working with artificial intelligence? You thought Amery brought you in to work on drone behavior? Come on," Lucas said.

"I didn't know, honestly. At first, that's all I was working with," Keith replied.

"I just...never thought Amery would resort to *this,*" Lucas said. Deep down, Keith knew Lucas' company could successfully contest the allegation that he was aware of the project's development involving human brain tissue, but he wanted him to keep quiet.

"This is where our research led us, Lucas. Amery wanted effectiveness. Seems we couldn't work around the human brain completely, it's far too valuable. Artificial intelligence wasn't what we needed."

"Who is he?" Lucas asked hesitantly.

"His name *was* Michael," Keith said, looking at the ground.

Michael was known as codename Saven to the people at SolarSystems Corporation. The fourteen-billion-dollar fusion of the most advanced technology humanity had to offer and alien reverse engineered Star Rust wreckage—the Experimental Cybernetic Humanoid Omega or E.C.H.O. as it was called.

"I'm guessing he doesn't answer to that name these days?" Lucas asked.

"Uh no. I can't say much, but I'll tell you he's from *here,* ironically. He grew up about seventy miles away from here, actually. Alaska-born and raised," Keith said.

"Home field advantage." Lucas raised his eyebrows.

"Yeah, it is. I hope anyway. Dr. Amery has assured me the man behind the mask willingly volunteered for the program, so I can say in full confidence everything has been handled," Keith said. He briefly recalled Michael's attempt to reject the program when he saw Vala's picture at the bank. Keith knew there was more to the story, but it wasn't necessary for Lucas to know everything.

"It just makes me wonder what his family would think if they saw him like *this.*" Lucas shook his head in disapproval.

"No family, just a fiancée," Keith said.

"Wow, you SolarSystems guys are hardcore. Even you. You didn't even flinch saying that," Lucas pointed out.

"No, it's not that. I just can't allow myself to think about it like that. I have a job to do and that's it," Keith replied.

"So why? Why would a man choose this?" Lucas said.

"His fiancée had a rare degenerative disease. Apparently, they couldn't afford surgery. The donor here had a severe accident himself, deforming much of his body. I'm guessing he didn't think he could take care of her, so he decided to donate. We paid his fiancée handsomely so she could afford the surgery. I would have done the same in his shoes," Keith said.

"That's easy to *say*," Lucas replied.

"Not for me," Keith said. He wondered if Lucas had any idea of his experience with his wife, not for sympathy reasons, but because he genuinely was a private person. Despite his attempts to keep it quiet, word always seemed to get around.

"He's former military?" Lucas asked.

"What makes you ask that?"

"Well, why would you want some regular Joe's brain? You'd want someone with highly specialized tactical training at the very least," Lucas said.

"Bingo. But he's more than just highly trained. Those are a dime a dozen. No offense. We narrowed it down from the very best candidates," Keith confirmed.

"None taken." Lucas shrugged.

"But that's all Amery wanted to keep from his brain— his training, innovativeness, and deciphering ability. Everything else was replaced," Keith said.

Keith was wrong about one thing. Amery directed his team to leave remnants of something else inside Michael's mind. Unbeknownst to Keith, Michael still had memories of Vala, left intentionally by Amery to give him drive and purpose.

After Michael begged Amery to let him see Vala again, he was emotionally traumatized and useless to the program. Amery and his people had to think quickly, so he directed his cerebral team to condition Michael to believe if he followed orders, he could see Vala again.

Michael was horrific. His head was a dark green, metal skull. His skin and hair removed in exchange for durable alien materials that fused into his bone. His human teeth had been removed, replaced only by two large metallic fangs that overhung from his upper jaw. A pair of dark holes were set where the eyes would normally be, casting an intimidating, vacant appearance. A coat of slimy residue from the stasis pod covered his face, dripping down from his canines.

"What's going on with the damn fangs? Those don't look like they're just for show?" Lucas asked.

"Not at all. His human jaw was replaced by a mechanical one that increases his range of motion. Also, his bite force is six times that of an African male lion. The two huge canines that protrude from his maxilla are titanium, three and a half inches in length and capable of poking holes through a human skull with ease."

"Shit... Well, he won't ever be in need of a nutcracker. You guys were definitely leaning toward a villain concept, huh? It reminds me of a cybernetic grim reaper with fangs, or something on the back of a biker's jacket." Lucas joked, attempting to calm himself.

"Fitting, I suppose. Not that many enemies would ever see him and live, but if that *did* happen, they probably wouldn't forget it, and that's what we want," Keith said, scanning the display on the pod.

"You want people to live and tell about it?" Lucas questioned.

"Fear. Echoing fear throughout the enemy ranks is something you can't reproduce. It's *the* exponential modifier in war. If the enemy is terrified, they're not operating to their capability." Keith said, pausing for a moment.

"Oh, *that's* how war works?" Lucas smirked.

"Well, you probably know something about getting in the enemy's head from your experience with the SEALS," Keith said confidently.

"A little bit, yeah," Lucas replied, nodding his head. Keith knew he'd never get any details out of him about it, but truthfully, he didn't want to know them. There were accusations in the media about Lucas' commando team's cruel behavior toward enemy soldiers during the beginning of the North Korean conflict.

"All right, I'm just going to boot him up and get him outside the pod so he can get in position. I need to check his vitals as well," Keith said as Lucas snapped his head around.

"WHOA...hold on. Whadaya mean, get him outside the pod? Like *right now*?" Lucas forced a smile. He was slightly crazy, but not stupid. He wasn't alone with his reaction.

SolarSystems actually had a few employees seek counseling over the new prototype. Most complained of nightmares, cold sweats, and anxiety while working around it. Keith was the only exception.

"Ha, the tables have turned. Just a few minutes ago, you were fondling human skulls, and now you're crapping your pants. It's completely fine, Lucas. I've worked with him for months. Also, I can shut him down with this, just in case." Keith held up a small thumb-sized device.

"Sure... yeah, go right ahead then buddy. Just keep your finger on that shutoff button," Lucas joked.

"Haha, all right...Here we go. Saven, active!" Keith's eyes gazed into the pod as it started the reboot process. A series of six white lights flickered from left to right like an old internet modem. The first light blinked a few times, then stayed on, then the second light did the same. Lucas weighed his options if things went south.

"This won't take long," Keith said, thinking about his explanation of fear and Lucas' reaction.

"That's comforting." Lucas smirked. "I was starting to get impatient."

No sooner than Lucas could finish talking, Saven raised his head inside the pod and his hybrid organic and machine lungs exhaled. It sounded like a rush of air and moisture being siphoned through a metallic filter. Condensation spotted up the pod's glass. Green lights slowly illuminated inside the once shadowy eye sockets.

"Oh, umm, yeah well, that's just fascinating isn't it," Lucas said, taking a step back. He turned around sizing up the exit.

Saven immediately fixed in on Lucas while in the pod, ignoring Keith. "Lucas, I'm going to ask you to calm down," Keith said.

"Oh, n-no. I'm fine. It's just... I was thinking I don't even have my sidearm," Lucas said excitedly, taking another step back.

"He knows you're nervous Lucas, so calm down. He can detect your heart rate and recognize the muscles in your face when they project fear, even when you attempt to hide it. Besides, a sidearm wouldn't help you anyway," Keith said.

Lucas frantically searched both directions of the corridor. "Once I get him out, you can't outrun him either." Keith smiled. "He'll run you down like a cheetah on a wounded gazelle. Relax."

"You coulda told me that earlier," Lucas said, wiping his forehead.

The pod's blacked-out glass shield rose automatically, but Saven took over. Clattering his long, spiny, metallic claws under the panel, he flipped the 160-pound lid open like a paperweight, rocking the pod back and forth from the force. The impact echoed down the corridor as Lucas gulped.

The dark green light inside the pod now illuminated his exposed body, instantly. "Oh shit." Lucas gushed with his eyes wide. What had started with Michael's legs was now a complete transformation. What remained of his body was fused together with jagged armored panels manifesting as a green and black exoskeleton.

"Saven, no hostiles detected. We're friendlies here," Keith said in a comforting tone.

Saven slowly extended one leg outside the pod. But to Lucas' surprise, it was no foot. A long, eagle-like metallic talon scraped the concrete ground as he peered left and right down the hall, ignoring Keith and Lucas. Saven reminded Keith of a captive animal being released back into the wild. Saven hunkered low, displaying a layer of caution mixed with excitement, ready to dart into the wilderness at a moment's notice.

His new form appeared long and lean, yet powerful and agile. The long, serrated, metallic wings on his back were folded in like two giant curved blades, highlighting a wicked, demonic form.

"We're still g-good, right? He's acting normal?" Lucas whispered.

"Yep, we're fine."

Between Saven's solar absorbing wings was a battery encased inside a vented housing. This kept him cool while simultaneously protecting his main power source, a battery that was powerful and rarely needed recharging.

The solar battery was special; only two were found in all the wreckage. SolarSystems' scientists couldn't figure out how to replicate its compact structure, so the battery was the actual unit extracted from the craft, minus the cleanup and protective housing.

Both were found on alien fighter jets that were possibly docked inside the massive starship during the crash. They provided incredible power with a ridiculously low input from solar rays.

Saven glanced at Keith, but focused back on Lucas. It seemed Saven understood Lucas wasn't an enemy, but he hadn't seen him before. Not to mention, the fear emitting from Lucas appeared to be exhilarating. Saven exited the pod, walking by Keith.

Saven's human posture had evolved also. He didn't stand completely upright, but always crouched down low, prepared for an explosive movement like a stalking cat. Suddenly, Saven took three quick steps, stopping inches in front of Lucas' face.

"Whoa, Lucas! Just don't move! It's fine, just a gesture of curiosity. He doesn't know you," Keith said. Lucas froze, dropping his arms to the side, unlocking his knees. Saven dipped his head around Lucas', attempting to sniff his fear, and basking in it for a moment.

Lucas' training kicked in, his heart rate spiked, but then began to stabilize. He shut his eyes, breathing in and out slowly. Lucas had narrowly escaped death before in battle, but he'd never looked into death's eyes until now. He was the very definition of pragmatic, yet here—Lucas was rattled.

"All right, that's enough, Saven. Sorry to wake you, but the exercise starts in a few hours. I thought I'd give you a chance to get in position and look at your surroundings," Keith said, examining the prototype for anything unusual. Saven's head snapped away from Lucas, walking slowly towards the exit, but he stopped parallel to Keith.

"Whew. Ah shit...He...*it* doesn't speak?" Lucas whispered.

"Nope. He receives orders and we monitor his systems constantly. If there's a problem, we'll know. He doesn't use verbal communication with us."

"Keith, it doesn't move like any machine I've ever seen. It's organic and fluid," Lucas examined.

Saven's head swiveled and snapped around like a bird of prey. His motion detection picked up on the rats scurrying about in the pitch-black corridor. Saven's numerous motion and heat sensors were perfectly synchronized with his heightened predatory instincts, providing him with a slew of target acquisition options.

"No, he doesn't really lean on his human instincts for movement anymore. That's all part of the UNIMEL system you're seeing. I'll explain it later. I was under a non-disclosure agreement until we got here, so I couldn't discuss its intricacies yet," Keith said.

Lucas nodded. There were always surprises with these tests, which was one of the perks of being able to witness them in the flesh.

"All right, Saven, your initial location is—that way." Keith paused then pointed down the hall. "I'll link the orders to your Heads-Up Display. You should be able to see the starting location zone...*now*," Keith said.

A location indicator popped up on Saven's map, giving him distance and route options.

Saven immediately lowered his body even farther. His shoulder blades bobbed up and down as he stalked like a cat through the damp hall on all fours slowly. Every several steps, he would raise up on his two legs, peering into the distance before dropping back down. Sometimes he would take a few steps on two legs, but it all transitioned smoothly, naturally.

"That's just bizarre, it's like blending a cat and man," Lucas said.

"And a bird. I guess I'm used to it, but I remember seeing it the first time as well."

Keith watched him disappear into the darkness. Eight months of training and billions of dollars' worth of research and development were on the line, but that wasn't it. To Keith, Saven was more than just a drone. He was part of Keith's recovery. Saven was a time sink that pulled him away from the demons of the past.

All of that was coming to an end though. This drill was the final stamp of approval for Saven before he was considered an active status unit. Keith thought about what he would do after the drill. More than likely, he'd have a lot of free time. So much of Saven's training had consumed his life, and it was a bit frightening to think about facing the past again.

"All right…ready to head back up?" Keith said.

"Yeah." Lucas replied casually.

"No need to pretend that you're not excited to get out of here."

"Great. I'll never hear the end of this one I'm sure." Lucas said, rolling his eyes. Keith walked over to the pod, closing the lid. "Oh shit!"

"What?!" Lucas asked.

"Oh… nothing… I just… the smell of the antibacterial gel hit me right in the face." Keith said, observing an image of a female face scratched into the interior of the pod. It was poorly drawn, almost a scribble. Keith stared at it for a few moments, glaring out towards Saven with his mouth open.

"Man, I would think you'd be used to that smell by now? I just held my breath," Lucas said.

"Yeah, I usually do, but sometimes I forget to."

"Right."

As they walked back topside, Lucas questioned Keith about the UNIMEL system and its inner workings. "He's more animal now, I'd guess, judging by his behavior?" Lucas asked.

"Ah, yeah. Ah, let's see here..." Keith replied, scratching his head.

"You ok? That smell got you, didn't it?

"Yeah. It can give you a headache... Ok... The way it works is pretty unique. UNIMEL technology is how we can attach certain animal instincts to Saven. One of the primary instincts is stalking, from the jaguar genes. As he moves, he automatically does things that people and drones don't," Keith said.

"Like what? Just movements or..." Lucas asked.

"I'll give you a small example. He can feel out the ground for things that could alert prey while stalking, like breaking a small branch. He would only apply a small amount of pressure first, gauging with his foot to see if it might make a noise. Then he would take the step, just like a jaguar. Small things like that can add up to a huge difference on the battlefield, as you know, especially against drones that have acute detections systems," Keith said.

Lucas listened attentively. It seemed as if he was associating the movements he had witnessed earlier to what he was hearing about Saven. His eyes lit up like a light bulb.

"Ah. I get it. It makes a lot of sense to me. Many of the guys in SEAL training were athletic, smart, and capable, but they still needed extensive training on how to be quiet. Even then, some of them were never really great at it. So yeah, that's a huge deal," Lucas gathered.

"I figured you would understand the importance better than most," Keith said.

"Yeah. You guys have dumped some serious man hours into this project. I mean, this is borderline insanity. I'm not sure how anyone would have the time to do... something like this," Lucas said.

"I wasn't finished..."

"Oh, excuse me, by all means, sorry to interrupt Doctor," Lucas said in a sarcastic tone. Keith rolled his eyes and smirked.

"The golden eagle is the other model we used. You probably observed much of it in his head movement."

"Yeah, he was looking all over the place. I didn't put it together that it was from a bird of prey, but now that you mention it..."

"Exactly, we wanted him alert to the smallest details. We combined that element of hyperawareness along with enhanced optics for picking up on targets at a distance. He's also likely to attack with those talons on his feet in close proximity, just like an eagle; keeping his vitals far away from reach. Also, he has a plasma saber on his wrist," Keith said.

"I thought you might use the bald eagle considering that's a symbol of the nation? Since you SolarSystems guys are raving patriots."

Keith rolled his eyes. "Funny. Well, we actually started to use the bald eagle, but studies showed the golden eagle was an aggressive solo predator, whereas the bald eagle was more of a scavenger."

"Really? Hmm. I would have never thought that. I used to wear an eagle on my chest every day. Never thought it was closer to a buzzard."

"Ha, well, I wouldn't go that far. I just think the golden eagle was the better choice for DNA instinct implementation."

"If you say so. Nothing screams warrior like eating food someone else killed," Lucas joked.

"Very effective tactic actually, just not for us. Anyway, those are just small examples of why we used the UNIMEL. The idea is that we can train people or drones to do those things. But having those attributes as they occur in *nature* is more efficient, and easier to integrate into a system with organic components. You're less likely to stray from your instincts," Keith concluded.

"Amazing engineering... I noticed the glowing compartment on his left forearm. That's the plasma saber's storage? That's from our findings?" Lucas asked.

"Yeah, we've made it a lot smaller for his application, but yes, the plasma saber, that's what we call it. It's a more compact version of the alien plasma weaponry for close quarters combat. It's about three feet long when extended. It cuts through titanium metal like butter," Keith said, shaking his head. "So imagine flesh and bone."

"That's disabled for the drill, right?" Lucas said.

"Oh my god, yes. There's no way we would allow him to use that even against the Marine drones. I just wouldn't want to risk it."

"The armor was our work too, right? The carbon fiber-like material?"

"More advanced as you know, but yes. The exoskeleton was designed from a military prototype we were working on, but we combined those alien materials you recovered from the Star Rust expeditions. We've used it more for lightweight strength in Saven's case. He's stronger than any man by far, but geared for speed first and foremost."

"Well, then, I can see why you only brought one," Lucas said, looking back down the long hall where Saven disappeared.

"I think we engineered from the absolute best human technology has to offer, along with enough alien technology to set him apart from anything ever seen before. There's more, but I'll get to that later," Keith said.

"I can't lie, you've sparked my interest, this is just baffling to me," Lucas said, scratching his head.

"I'm sure you've seen things out on your expeditions that would make me ooze with curiosity."

"I cannot confirm or deny, yada yada, all of that," Lucas smiled.

"Uh huh," Keith replied.

"So, now we're just waiting on the Washington suits to arrive?" Lucas questioned.

"They should be arriving anytime now."

The next phase of the Crucible was the arrival of the evaluators. Agents and their supporting elements were arriving from Washington, DC from an unknown intelligence agency. Their job was twofold: assess the prototype's performance and mediate between Keith as a representative of SolarSystems and the US Marines.

They arrived with their own security: thirty-two guards, six observers, and four pilots for both transports that stayed onsite. They were the only people on base allowed to carry live ammunition.

The Marines and Saven's weaponry were replaced with stun rounds that sent a signal to command. If Saven was struck once, that was it. For testing, Saven's weapons automatically switched to stun when he reached a certain proximity to the Marines or pointed his weapon at a human.

The Washington element arrived in two of the same Wraith-style jets as the Marines. They were all black instead of gray and had a partial cloaking device enabled.

Their engines generated about half the decibels too. They got the bulk of the tax dollars compared to the Marines.

The 0700 meeting the next morning was too early for everyone, even the Marines. Each party was given a rude awakening when the cold morning air hit them. It seemed the heating system gave out at around 0400 and kept most people awake and freezing.

The Marines slowly filed out into the courtyard with Keith and Lucas intermingled between them. They met up on the opposite side of the courtyard in formation. Keith saw one of the Marines from the previous Crucible he'd somehow missed earlier.

"Hey, Sergeant Martin. How'd you sneak in here?" Keith joked, shaking his hand.

"Ah, well, you know how it is. I was probably doing some of the bitch work and you must have missed me." Martin smiled.

"Ha! It's good to see you again." Keith nodded and clapped his shoulder. About that time, Belmont turned around, glancing at both Martin and Keith. He cut his eyes away in disapproval.

"Associating with the enemy, huh?" Lucas leaned in.

"Yeah." Keith rolled his eyes, smiling. He didn't have a problem with Martin. He'd met him last year during the Crucible. He seemed like a troubled, but solid individual. Keith had the feeling Belmont had it out for him, but he never asked why.

Keith could see the agents ahead. They seemed to be assessing the situation, despite the drill not having started yet. Keith checked his watch with a small holographic display, revealing Saven had reached his position and was on standby.

Good. All right, we're ready. Breathe.

Keith took in a big breath as two government agents strutted out to the front of the group along with six armed guards. They looked across the Marine ranks and paused for a brief moment.

"Marines and the parties from SolarSystems. Welcome to the Crucible. I am Agent Casser, and this is my associate, Agent Niven." He gestured towards his younger partner with a smile.

Casser was an average looking fellow, short with thinning hair on top and a huge burn scar across the left side of his face. He seemed intelligent and highly skeptical, if not overly critical. That was part of the reason he was in his position.

His associate, Niven, was younger. Tall and thin with dark skin and a typical agent's clean-cut look. Unlike Casser, his eyes were wide and his grin seemed forced. He crossed his arms in front of him while tapping his index finger on his gloves erratically.

The Marines immediately began to mock the agents under their breath, low enough in volume so that several of the others could hear it but the agents couldn't.

"Haha. Look at this guy's hair."

"Right? Hey, bro, no shame in wearing a cap in this weather," a Marine joked from the back of the ranks.

Unfortunately, Captain Belmont was one of those Marines that heard the joke. He turned around to address it while the agent spoke. "Do *we* have a problem, Marines?" Belmont demanded, daring any Marine to snicker again.

Casser paused politely and smirked. He held his crossed arms in front of his chest, allowing Belmont time to control his men before continuing on.

"Everything okay? Great... All right, first things first. This objective-based war game is designed to test cohesion of our Marine tactical units and our newest prototype. First and foremost, we are *all* on the same side," Casser said, pausing for a moment to scan across the faces and send that point home.

Lucas, Keith, and his technicians stood opposite of the Marines in the courtyard with a modest spacing of about ten paces between them. There wasn't any worry of physical aggression, but there was definitely tension, reputation, and billions of dollars of research on the line.

"Okay, let me see... Captain Belmont?" Casser called out.

"Yes, sir," Belmont rogered up in a low but deep voice, raising his hand. It wasn't difficult to spot him in the crowd.

"Right. Uh, phase one will be perimeter engagements, as you know. For the ones who don't, listen up. The SolarSystems prototype will be pitted against the Marines' arsenal of drones and sensors. Lethal force is permitted here on both sides, drones against the prototype. Obviously, no persons will be involved in this portion of the drill."

Lucas turned his head slowly, glaring over at Keith. "None that *they* know of, anyway," he whispered.

Keith bit his bottom lip.

"We'll be on station to shut down the drill to prevent anything from going overboard, but this is a high stakes situation," Casser said.

Keith gulped. He felt his heart racing. Not only were Lucas and himself the only people there that knew Saven was part human, but Keith had formed an attachment with Saven. These Marines were trying to kill someone he'd trained and watched progress for months.

"Seriously, Keith?" Lucas whispered.

Keith simply looked straight ahead at Casser, ignoring the question.

Casser spoke before Keith could answer. "This first phase of the games will be far enough away that we aren't at risk. We'll be underground. The Marines will control and send out their drones to hunt down the *intruder*. We have a kill switch for every drone as a fallback, correct?" Casser questioned.

"Yes, sir. All of them," Belmont answered quickly.

"Of course, Agent Casser. I can power the prototype down as well, if needed. I'll link your team with access," Keith said.

"Good. We'll need access to that capability on both sides," Casser ordered.

Belmont smirked. The rumor was that this newest prototype might be more of a challenge, but supposedly, so was the last one. What better way to prove his effectiveness as a leader than to deliver a knockout blow in the first phase?

Not only that, Captain Belmont was up for the rank of major. A decisive win against SolarSystems just might push him over the edge this time.

Casser continued with the briefing. "Phase two will be Marines versus the prototype. All Marine and prototype firearms will be set to stun rounds. In this phase, the prototype must infiltrate command and assassinate the terrorist leader, which, in this case, will be played by you, Mr. Belmont," Casser said as the Marines looked right at him. Belmont had already made it clear the prototype wouldn't even make it to this stage of the drill, and that was an order, not an opinion.

"Phase two starts when and if the prototype makes it within a two-mile radius of this installation. Phase one is anything beyond that marked two-mile radius," Casser briefed.

Before starting again, Casser looked toward Garza, a veteran of these games. He'd seen Garza in at least two previous Crucibles. Garza nodded at him when they made eye contact. Casser returned the gesture respectfully while speaking.

Staff Sergeant Garza was the only female in the unit, but by far, the most capable leader other than Belmont and easily the best shooter. A true professional. She was about five foot nine and built athletically. She didn't say much, but when she did, it stuck. She thought about her words and her actions before executing.

She demanded respect. Not once did she ever receive a sexual advance from one of her fellow Marines—a common issue in most coed platoons such as this.

It wasn't because she lacked physical appeal. She was an attractive tomboy, but she made it clear she didn't date Marines and they listened.

Garza was from deep in south Texas. She grew up during a violent war between the drug lords and the authorities. Two of her uncles and an aunt were killed in the vicious battles for control over the border.

Garza learned to use a gun at the age of ten. Since she could remember, it had been nothing but fighting. By the age of twelve, she was on guard duty outside of her window with an old-school AK-100 rifle, watching her neighborhood.

Surges of violence spilled over the border, then subsided. The fighting peaked at one point, forcing the president to send in the Marines. He didn't bother with the National Guard. The Marines quickly dispatched the thugs, driving them back into Mexico and setting up camp in her hometown for a few months. Garza was impressed by the Marines' camaraderie and take-charge attitude. Even though she was only in middle school, she decided then that was what she wanted to do.

"Marines, obviously, your goal is to repel the assassin and protect Captain Belmont. Any contact shot will count as a death for either side, forcing you to sit out the remainder of the games in our penalty box."

"If you manage to shoot the prototype *once*, you win. No questions asked. Friendly fire counts as a death too," Casser said, nodding his head slightly.

"Ah man, all we gotta do is hit that thing once? Seems a little unfair. We'll have twenty-two rifles on him. He won't even make it past our drones," an older corporal joked.

Belmont and Garza both turned slowly toward the outburst.

"You done?" Garza said. The corporal lowered his head slightly, pretending he didn't notice them staring.

"All right, the games start at exactly 1300 hours today. I understand the Marines have set up their drone stations and are ready, as is the prototype. We will be in the control center, monitoring all communications and cameras." Casser looked around briefly then paused.

"If there are any questions during the event or medical emergencies, use channel 01. That's where we will be. You have your orders. Good luck." Casser dashed back toward his station, pointing his men in various directions.

"Keith, lethal force for phase one?" Lucas questioned again as they headed back. Keith was visually upset, trying to appear focused, but it didn't work.

"Yeah... well, they think he's a drone, that's why. They think we can just replace the parts, but..." Keith said as Lucas stepped out in front of him.

"Can't replace a person," Lucas pointed out as the Marines marched past them. Some of them brushed up against Keith while giving Lucas room.

"That's not going to happen. There's a reason I've poured my life into this, and I'll be damned if anyone takes it away from me. This is our moment, and whatever happens, at least I can say I put my all into it," Keith said intensely. He lowered his voice as Garza stomped towards them.

"Excuse me, gentlemen," Garza said, turning her body sideways and stepping between them.

"You've done *more* than enough, Keith. I've never seen anyone this devoted to any program, but—" Lucas said.

"What then? That's it," Keith replied.

"There's something morally wrong here. Don't you feel it? I understand he's not completely human. I get that." Lucas paused.

"There's not much morally *right* about the world these days. You of all people ought to understand that. No offense. I can't help that I'm on this side of it now. I just hope some good can come from it," Keith explained. Lucas stared at Keith for a few seconds.

"That's what I used to tell myself," Lucas said as trudged off.

Keith looked crestfallen at Lucas' remarks. However, there was a certain strength emitting from his demeanor. Deep down, he was fighting back. It was a mental war he wasn't going to take lying down.

He understood Lucas could recognize that in his eyes. He knew Lucas had experiences in the SEALs he wasn't proud of. He'd probably lost some men.

Keith knew the other side of it. Risking Saven in a drill did seemed pointless, but his development had always been about a victory at the Crucible. It wasn't war, it was a drill, and despite the prototype being mostly machine, he was still part man.

However, to some, it was worth the risk. If Saven could be successful here, he'd most certainly land a government contract that paid back the investment tenfold. It wouldn't be easy though. The Crucible was designed for failure. A Marine element team stacked with experience against a single prototype. The odds were not in Saven's favor.

Chapter Ten

Agent Casser booted up all his command room cameras. The system was cutting edge, for the mid-2060s at least, but it was due for an upgrade. He'd been using this same setup since the Crucible started. That was before SolarSystems was even conceived.

He wondered when he would get funding for newer holographic 3D cameras that could see through walls. For now, he could see and hear most everything, Saven's perspective, the drone's, Keith's control room, and all the Marine stations. He had eyes and ears everywhere down to the smallest detail.

"Well, people, we have a visual..." Casser said as their cameras displayed images and audio. Agent Niven came in and sat down beside him, giving him a tally of agents watching the various cameras, including himself.

"Did anyone bring popcorn?" Niven joked.

"This is serious business. If we miss something, it could be dangerous," Casser said, sternly looking at Niven. Casser leaned in, whispering, "That's not the example I want to set for our newest agents, not that *you* are seasoned, by any means."

"I understand, sir. Just trying to lighten the mood a bit."

One hour before the drill, Casser observed Keith and Lucas glaring over at the Marines. The old, misty glass window that separated the two parties was blurred, but they could still see each other.

The Marines came alive. They moved quickly and with purpose, like an army of ants rising up to protect the hill from an intruder. Everyone had a role that appeared second nature, drilled in over hundreds of hours of repetition.

"Icepick, this is bravo actual. How copy?" the Marine prompted his drone.

The drone's artificial intelligence pinged back a "Ready" flash on the operator's holographic display.

The drones had an intimidating stance, tank-like tracks for movement, twin laser cannons on each arm that were gyro-stabilized, and a basketball-sized sensor array for a head. The brutes were clearly the seek-and-destroy element for the Marines.

"Copy that, Icepick. Proceed to phase one starting location. How copy?" The drone moved in for the closest possible jump on the prototype.

Icepick was the lead brute drone. Even if communications were somehow severed, Icepick could order the other brutes strategically without human intervention and was linked to five other subordinate drones.

Icepick had a series of notches all down his left and right laser cannons, each notch confirming a kill in the North Korean war. A yellow notch indicated an enemy drone kill and red for a human kill. The tally seemed to be about even, with slightly more organic kills than machine, but he was running out of room on both sides.

The other brute drones seemed fairly new by comparison to Icepick. They had shiny white armor panels, brand new guns, and only a few yellow notches here and there scattered between them.

Each brute formed a linked spherical radius of sensors that blanketed Saven's route to the installation. Casser watched the Marines grow more excited by the second.

"Just like the last Crucible, their prototype can't move past these sensor zones without us knowing it. Once it crosses, it's over," Garza said to one of her newer Marines, pointing at the screen.

"Let's hope their prototype is aggressive and we can leave that much sooner," Belmont chimed.

"That sensor zone trap gets Solarsystems almost every time," Casser said, shaking his head.

"Wonder why SolarSystems doesn't alter their tactics?" Niven asked.

"There's not really much they can do."

"Why?" Niven asked.

"Well, as you know, drones emit an electronic signature, a beacon... Unless they can find a way to mask it." Casser shrugged.

"Alright, countdown to the Crucible in fifteen minutes. We're live in fifteen..." Agent Casser paged throughout the installation. Each party alerted their assets of the timer.

Casser watched Saven's mounted camera from the control room, as did Lucas and Keith in their station. It was difficult to tell what Saven was doing, his camera was facing down, like he was scaling a mountain.

"He's moving nearly forty miles an hour now," Lucas observed his statistics onscreen.

"That's uphill and in heavy snow," Keith replied.

Lucas observed closely, moving his seat closer to the monitor, as did Keith. They could see Saven's talons and legs flicker and disappear as they churned through the snow.

"Is that a glitch in the camera feed? Look at his talons." Lucas observed.

"He's cloaking. Yes, the wing-like structure on his back can conform to most any shape or color. It can cover his entire body for concealment or even fan out like an actual set of wings for gliding. We call them shards," Keith explained.

"So he would have to drop his cloak to glide?" Lucas questioned.

"Yeah, if he's using the shards to glide, obviously they're not covering his body. So no camouflaging nor armor. He has to decide when to use them," Keith concluded. The camera above Keith and Lucas had a small red light blinking on it, indicating that Casser's team was listening in.

"Hmm, interesting. I don't like that Solarsystems' prototype is limited by using armor or stealth, seems like a lot of decision making on the fly," Niven noted.

"How is a machine supposed to dynamically figure out which to use?" Casser questioned suspiciously. He watched Niven as a light bulb went off in his head.

"Maybe they have an advanced form of artificial intelligence? Or... maybe it's being remote controlled from an offsite location?" Niven posed.

"Could be," Casser said, poking out his bottom lip.

Keith continued explaining it to Lucas while the agents listened in. "For instance, now, when cloaking, his fingertips analyze the properties of the terrain he's touching, and he can project that color scheme throughout his body. Right now, he's using white like the snow obviously," Keith said, rubbing his own fingers together while explaining it.

"And armor is the third option."

"Ah, I was wondering about this," Lucas replied.

"Yeah. The shards in this mode are doubled up around his vitals and sensors, providing extra protection," Keith said.

"Hopefully, he won't need that here," Lucas sighed.

Keith glared at Lucas. "God, I hope not. We could have gone with a technology that allowed for all three simultaneously, but weight was a huge issue and we want him ultra-fast and agile," Keith said.

An armed guard patrolled the hall between Solarsystems and the Marines. Even in these war games, Marines were known to be aggressive to the competition. Some of them were even wearing war paint, so taking things too lightly was not a concern.

Casser leaned in toward the mic. "Everyone is in position, starting in three... two... one... It's a go! We are live fire, people," Casser signaled over the installation's old speaker box. "Good luck to both elements. Let's be safe."

"Ooo-Rah!" the younger Marines shouted out as the drill started. Some of them had been training months for this moment, and it was probably the closest thing to combat they'd seen.

"I don't know why Casser uses that speaker box. Plenty of other ways to get in touch. He used that old relic in the last Crucible too," Garza said, rubbing her neck.

"Sounds like an old battleship's 1MC intercom from the movies," Belmont joked. "He probably loves this shit. Sitting up there, looking down on all the action. He's probably got popcorn and snuggled up in a blankey," Belmont said. Garza and some of the other Marines around them laughed.

"Do they not understand we can hear them?" Casser questioned, throwing his hands up.

"I'm not sure they care, sir," Niven said, looking away.

Belmont pointed toward the operator's stations. "Alright, let's go." Garza was responsible for half of the computer stations as an overseer while Belmont took the others, dividing the responsibility. Their control room was set up in a "U" formation with an island monitor in the middle that allowed either overseer to take control as a drone operator or safety coordinator.

"Icepick, move forward and maintain course at ninety degrees," Garza ordered.

Lucas peered through the heavy snow onscreen as Saven came to a stop at the top of the mountain. His breath wisped in the air as he panned around like a bird of prey stalking rodents.

"Sniping angle?" Lucas said, watching Saven's feed.

"No idea," Keith said. "He seems more exposed up there honestly."

"You're just nervous. It's natural. Listen, I've been up against some of the most terrifying weapons man has ever created, and I would not want to be on the opposite side of what you've concocted here," Lucas said, injecting a bit of confidence.

"Well, coming from a Navy SEAL, I guess that's not bad."

"A SEAL with plenty of experience against attack drones," Lucas said.

Keith sighed loudly, pulling his hair back while standing. He walked back and forth around the room, glancing at the camera every couple of seconds.

Back over on the Marine's side, Belmont paced the room too, scowling at each operator's screen intensely. Once in a while, he'd pass a Marine and pat him on the back with a, "You good?"

"Make sure you keep an eye out. Just because we have sensors doesn't mean we should ignore the human element. Watch your video feed. That's why it's there. Use your eyes, that's why God gave them to ya." Belmont smiled, showing a mouth full of pearly white teeth seldom seen by his subordinates.

Casser peered over at the veteran drone Icepick's camera. He was moving above the maximum speed listed for a brute.

"You know why the Marines call him Icepick?" Casser questioned as his crew watched on.

No one said anything. They just stared at Casser, waiting for a response.

"It's like this weather doesn't' affect him. He's singlehandedly accumulated the most prototype kills out here in this snow. It's like home field advantage for him. The Marines usually keep him in and around the snow."

"Why would a drone prefer snow over another setting? That doesn't make any sense," Niven questioned with a puzzled look on his face.

"Why does any person prefer the snow over any other setting? That doesn't make sense. You'd have to be insane to like it over a beach in my opinion, but hey, there are plenty of people out there that do," Casser pointed out.

"But he's a drone."

"So? People need heat to survive, yet many like being out in the freezing cold. Icepick doesn't require much heat at all. I don't know why, just like I don't know why people do. Artificial Intelligence has its quirks, just as people do."

Agent Niven laughed. "Okay."

They watched on as Icepick burrowed through a set of drifts. His terrain navigation alerted him of possible route hazards and his fellow brute's status. Every so often, he would stop to assess movement or heat signatures.

Icepick focused in on a set of footprints in the snow just ahead. It was difficult to assess exactly what the footprints were from because snow had covered over them somewhat. Icepick scanned, setting a course to follow. He tracked them up a slight incline then down into a valley with hills on both sides.

Suddenly, everyone in the Marine control room froze. Icepick had pointed his twin cannons ahead, scoping in on something in the distance.

Shoof Shoof Shoof Shoof

"Icepick is firing. Icepick is firing!" A corporal yelled as muffled electronic pulsing sounds rattled out, echoing off the landscape.

"What do we have people?!" Belmont yelled. Both him and Garza rushed over to the display to observe the action.

"Oh. Already?" Casser evaluated his cameras.

"What do you see? Any visual?" Belmont questioned. Casser noticed Belmont's fingers on the desk as he hunched over the operator's shoulder. It appeared as if he was clawing the desk in anticipation.

"Staff Sergeant Garza, over here," Belmont ordered her to his display. "See the top of this ridge way out in the distance? It's as if something is masking an electronic signature up there. It's definitely not natural. I'm sending two additional brutes to this position ASAP."

"Agreed. That's definitely odd. We need to get closer though," Garza said.

Belmont pulled up a holographic map of his brute drones, tapping the interface to redirect his forces.

"I see their drones! But, Saven's just…staring at them! Why?" Keith said, biting his nails.

"Hold on." Lucas replied.

"All operators, I'm sending two additional brutes to Icepick's position to investigate an electronic signal masking. Icepick, stand by before you proceed. How copy, over?" Belmont instructed over the comms.

Drones B2 and B3 quickly converged on Icepick's position. To save time, the drones intercepted Icepick's exact route to avoid deciphering environmental hazards themselves, as Icepick's route was already confirmed safe.

"ETA seven minutes on backup. Sit tight, Icepick," Garza said.

Keith and Lucas could only speculate what was happening. They would glance across the hall at the Marines as if they were up to something.

Their body language had changed. They were more hurried and excited for some reason. Lucas got out of his chair, peering out through the misty glass panels.

"Any ideas?" Keith asked.

"Seems like they've found a blood trail over there," Lucas assessed, raising his eyebrows.

"Terrible choice of words, Lucas."

"Yeah. Sorry 'bout that. To be clear he's not injured from what I can tell." Lucas said. Keith snapped his head around at him. "Thanks."

Agent Casser chuckled. "I don't think we've ever seen Keith this worried. He should be used to losing Crucibles by now."

"All right, drones B2 and B3 have reached Icepick. Proceed to the anomaly?" Garza questioned.

Belmont took one last look at his digital map. "Yes. We have numbers on our side. Operators, glue your eyes to that screen. Move forward in formation. Just like we've trained, people. Remember CCS."

The *Constant Cycle of Sensors* was the phrase used to remind Marines to continually toggle across all camera modes and sensors to obtain the most dynamic assessment. No one form of intelligence trumped them all.

Icepick pushed forward, leading out in front of the other two drones by about twenty meters, creating a "V" formation. Sitting in the snowstorm had nearly buried Icepick's tracks. The operator increased the throttle to maximum just to dig through the heap.

"Snow's picking up!" Garza yelled across the room.

The snow had changed directions too. It came directly toward the drones now, dotting the operator's camera feed.

"Can't see much, but we're getting close to the signal," Garza said. "B2, move ahead of Icepick fifteen meters and switch to automated, motion-sensing guns."

"Left forty-eight degrees, B2. What's that?" Garza zoomed in on something up about sixty meters high on a mountain.

"Everyone, fix in on that position. There's definitely something up there," Belmont ordered. "Move a little closer, B2. We can't get a visual with all this damn snow."

Garza took over B2's camera, zooming in on the object. It was protruding out from the hillside in an unusual manner. She switched from IR scope to sonar, and then back to normal.

"That's definitely not right. That anomaly is blurring between visual modes," Garza said.

"That? What the hell?" Belmont pointed over Garza's shoulder at the holographic interface.

Suddenly, a set of green eyes flashed and the blurred object vanished over the hill. The explosive movement caused B2's motion guns to open fire, chasing the hazed figure into the white mist. Icepick and B3 joined in on B2's solo performance, scorching the mountainside with a symphony of laser fire.

"Yeah, kill it!" B2's operator chanted as the rest of the room gasped.

"Maybe this drill is over before it even started?" Belmont said, panning across the room and smirking.

Steam trailed into the horizon from the vaporized snow, followed by the sound of rumbling. It sounded like a distant downpour.

"Wait… oh, no…" Belmont's eyes widened. "Retreat! Back 'em up, back 'em up! Go! Go! Go!"

His voice thundered across the hall as Keith and Lucas snapped over at the commotion. Both jumped up.

"Look!" Keith yelled. Steam was venting into Saven's face as the ground shook beneath him.

Suddenly, a tidal wave of snow cascaded downward. Giant chunks of ice and rocks stampeded toward the drones as they attempted to escape. Icepick darted under a small chasm as drones B2 and B3 turned and churned in retreat.

B3 was lagging behind. Its Marine operator could only watch as it was tattered. The camera feed tumbled, flickered, and then blacked out as they were buried under the tsunami of snow.

Saven leaped onto the largest chunk of ice, sinking his talons into it. He rode down the avalanche, projecting his wings across himself like a protective shell, shielding his vital systems as he descended.

"What?! I can't watch. This isn't happening." Keith said with a pale face.

Lucas watched as the ground rapidly approached, but at the last second, Saven sprung off the boulder. He fanned out his shards into a winged formation, gliding above drone B2 like a bird of prey looming over a rodent.

As Saven sailed closer, he tucked his wings in tight around his frame, dipping head first to increase speed. Just before impact, he rolled feet first, daggering his claws toward the fleeing drone. Sparks ejected into the air on contact as he plunged his talons into the brute's dome-like head. He twisted his body around in mid-flight, pulling the drone's head off and flinging it across the ice. The head was attached to a spine-like array of connectors and wires, now strewn across the ice chaotically.

"What happened?! It can fly?!" Belmont shouted.

Saven landed on a knee a dozen meters ahead of the drone, his metallic wings draped over him, sprawling across the snow. The downed drone was crumpled upside down behind him, its engine hummed while the tank-like tracks spun aimlessly in the air.

"One down!" Lucas yelled. Keith peeked through his fingers. "Really?"

"Yeah."

Gunfire erupted near Saven's position, but he instinctively dove into the snow. "No! I was hoping the avalanche got the other two." Keith said with his hands atop his head.

"Something's off about this one though. Look." Lucas pointed at the drone's upper torso as it jolted about erratically, searching for a target. Keith squinted his eyes, "damaged, good, that'll help us."

Saven peeked his head up like a lurking snow leopard. He cautiously reached out for a fragment of debris, cupping it in his hand. Saven observed the drone as it scanned back and forth, then tossed the debris over it. The drone's guns tracked the object, opening fire and destroying it.

"Oh, ok. I think that drone's basically blind other than motion sensors." Keith observed. Saven burrowed through the snow, stalking as low as possible.

Surprisingly, Saven moved back toward the flipped over drone, B2. As he approached, Lucas and Keith could hear its tracks spinning loudly in the air.

"Why is he going back? He's already taken out that drone?" Keith asked.

"I uh, I think he has an idea." Lucas smirked. Saven overturned B2 right side up. It's spinning tracks dug in, immediately launching it in the direction of B3's motion sensors.

Saven flanked around wide, opposite of B3's firing line. B3 began firing on his comrade, ripping the remainder of the drone apart until it exploded. Keith flashed a full smile, nodding his head with pride.

Saven barreled full speed at the distracted drone and pounced on its back. He clutched the drone underneath its arms, out of range from its deadly cannons. Saven unlocked his powerful mechanical jaw, he opened wide, thrusting his massive fangs deep into the drone's upper neck. He viciously tore into its sensors as a motorized wince shrieked out from the helpless drone.

"This is just, brutal." Lucas mumbled with his wide eyes.

The drone spun around in circles erratically, attempting to toss the attacker, but Saven rodeoed the brute. With each second, he ripped deeper into its workings, crunching away mouthfuls of vital robotic wreckage until nothing remained but a heap of scrap.

"Two down!" Keith pumped his fist.

"That was sort of hard to watch, like those old nature documentaries where the big cat kills its struggling prey." Lucas joked. Back in Casser's control room, the display was met with skepticism.

"Ok, now that was unexpected, you said Solarsystems never did anything to speak of, this is either an extraordinary piece of hardware, or they're cheating? Maybe there's an offsite operator?" Niven rattled, squinting his eyes.

"Have you checked to see if having a remote operator is a violation of the rules?" Casser grinned.

"Section 29-4 clearly states that remote operators aren't allowed," Niven immediately answered.

"What about our sensors? Are you picking up any encrypted signals being broadcasted?"

"Uhh, let's see. No, nothing at all, actually," Niven said, confused.

"I can't believe that just happened." Lucas said under his breath.

"We've never taken out a brute, those things have been impossible to kill." Keith said.

"We just got two of them." Lucas replied.

Keith sat down, rocking back and forth in his chair enthusiastically. It wasn't a completed work of art, but it was a beautiful draft thus far. Even if the drill ended now, it was further than anyone had made it against these Marines.

Suddenly, a loud boom erupted across the hall. Keith and Lucas glared toward the Marines' control room.

The reaction wasn't quite as positive across the hall. Apparently, Belmont had kicked drone B2's screen display, destroying it. Pieces of glass and plastic littered the floor. He exited the room, yelling and cursing.

The Marine control room was awkwardly silent. One of the corporals had buried his face in his hands and removed his earpiece. His drone was down. In Belmont's unit, the Marine was responsible for losing his or her drone.

"Marines, our data tells us you lost two brute drones. Is that correct?" Agent Casser questioned over the loudspeaker.

"Two?" Suddenly, Garza jumped over to Icepick's station. The drone was damaged severely but operational. His detection sensors, cameras, and cannons were destroyed, but his tracks and automated navigational systems were functional.

"Confirmed, two down, that means Icepick is operational." Keith tilted his head at the loudspeaker.

"I can't help but wonder what's going through Belmont's mind right now. Those brutes are battlefield beasts, and your science project here just took out two of them without firing a shot." Lucas said.

"Science project." Keith shook his head.

Belmont stormed back into his control room. "Everyone at attention. NOW!"

The Marines instantly snapped up out of their stations at full attention. Belmont circled around the room, not saying a word before he glared at each person.

Belmont's uniform appeared sloppy and his forehead was sweaty. He was clearly a man with a lot to lose. His reputation was on the line.

"Does anyone here know how many brute drones we've lost in combat in the last three years?" Belmont questioned.

Garza knew the answer, but stayed quiet.

"Two. We've lost two brutes in combat in the last three years. We just lost two in fourteen minutes," Belmont said. He paused then started pacing, allowing that information to sink in.

"I don't know what this thing is. Don't care. All I know is it will not make it to phase two. Is that understood?"

"Ooh Rah!" The Marines masked their uncertainty with that ancient battle cry.

"Everyone back on station now. What's our status?" Belmont questioned.

"We still have three fully operational brutes, sir, and Icepick is at least…functional," a corporal answered.

"Icepick won't go down that easily." Belmont checked the display's status of the veteran drone.

"Well, get him back here, now. The longer he's out there, the more vulnerable he is. Basically, he's just a set of tracks and sensors."

"Sir, you really think he has a chance of making it back?" Garza questioned, furrowing her eyebrows skeptically.

"Nah, I don't, but we're not just leaving him out there either."

"Roger that." She said.

"We're going to fill the holes that drones B2 and B3 left. The prototype will try to shoot through their radar zone gap, if it's smart," Belmont explained.

Twilight set across the frozen woodland. The wind let up as the light snow fell straight down, almost in a drizzle. The intensity in the Marine control room subsided as well, allowing everyone to collect their thoughts and relax.

The Marines had set up a series of massive LED lights that lit up the perimeter like a football stadium. The two operators that lost their drones went out to assist by placing more sensor traps, just in case Saven's "luck" or "bad weather" streak continued.

Chapter Eleven

Lucas yawned. "I'm going to hit the rack. I'll be back up here early in the morning. You need anything?"

"Nah, I'm good," Keith answered, staring at Saven's vitals. His camera was completely black. For some reason, it wasn't functioning properly. "Did Saven disconnect his camera?" Keith mumbled.

"What?" Lucas asked.

"Um, nothing, just trying to get this camera back online."

"Man. Heck of a day," Lucas said before exiting.

"Yeah, it could have been worse, right?" Keith smiled.

As Lucas left, Keith pulled out his personal tablet and made a few notes to himself about the drill along with some remote diagnostic reminders for the next day.

The clock rolled over to midnight, and the date changed to January 22nd. It was his ninth anniversary with his late wife, Olivia. He raised his eyebrows, surprised by the realization. He'd been working so hard on getting Saven ready that he didn't realize their anniversary had rolled around.

"Oh. Nine years. Gosh."

He had a tradition every year since she'd passed away. It wasn't anything elaborate, but to him it was special. He uploaded a video file from his documents titled "Oli and me."

He opened the file, and hesitated before pressing play, but he did. The video started where Keith proposed to Olivia. He took her to their favorite vineyard in California. The same one they'd gone to on their first date. Keith had his best friend Charlie record the whole thing from afar.

"This is it. Don't choke, buddy," he said, watching from a parked car. Keith kept his silly grin on the whole time.

The video portrayed Keith taking a knee, staring up into her green eyes. Her light blue dress blew in the breeze toward him. The file's audio wasn't perfect with all the wind, but Keith remembered the words, so he whispered them aloud, in sync with the video.

"A long time ago, we came here as strangers. Now, the time has come for me to ask you to be my love, forever. I promise to protect you, love you, and care for you until the day I die. Olivia Reiner… w-will you marry me?" Keith said. His eyes watered, but he had a big smile on his face.

"Yes… Yes, I will," she said. A few stragglers from the vineyard started clapping as she placed her hand over her mouth.

Keith's bottom lip quivered. "I didn't protect her though." Keith shut his eyes, putting his hands over his face. He wept uncontrollably.

When Michael showed up at SolarSystems, Keith initially saw him as just another project.

But Michael was different. When Keith heard about his sacrifice, he identified with that. In a small way, he felt that he and Michael were a lot alike. Both were willing to do whatever it took to protect the ones they loved. Keith drew strength from the idea that if he were given the chance to sacrifice himself for his family, he would. Just like Michael did.

To Keith, a part of himself lived on in Saven. He symbolized that drive to carry on despite tragedies in life. The tenacity to push forward. To pick yourself up, no matter what pieces remained, and fight. To Keith, Saven wasn't a wasted life.

Keith walked back down to the pod later, opening the lid slowly. He closed his eyes before peering inside, hoping he'd imagined what he saw previously. He opened his eyes, and there it was, the female face chiseled into the metal.

"Dammit!" He ran his hands over it. The thing had been scratched in by Saven's claws. He stared it at for several moments, shaking his head in confusion, "How? Maybe it's just a flash memory, coincidence, or random? I don't know. Never seen that before." Keith mumbled to himself.

"Let's   just   get   through   the   damn   drill."

Chapter Twelve

Lucas was escorted back to his quarters, considering the drill was in active status. An agency guard walked him past the Marines as Belmont cut his eyes at him.

"The Marines aren't going to sleep?" Lucas questioned the guard.

"They're taking shifts, but are on call and can be on full alert at a moment's notice. You know how it is, sir." Lucas did a double take at the guard. He guessed he was ex-military. He just had the look. He had those faraway eyes that never completely unglued from some event set in his past.

"So, what are you, ex...what?" Lucas asked.

"Air Force. Scorns," the guard replied. He had that look too, one couldn't fake—modest, with cold eyes, but tough as nails.

"Really? Huh, this sort of duty is a bit... *grounded* for you, isn't it?" Lucas joked as the guard laughed.

"Ha, indeed it is, sir. That's exactly how I like it these days though," the mid-forties Scorn replied. But anything was grounded for that soldier. Even though they didn't have the full capability to explore the galaxy yet, the Scorns were the first operational soldiers trained specifically for space combat within our solar system.

"Right, well, I hope this isn't too boring for you. Have a good night. Maybe something exciting will happen," Lucas said as they approached his quarters.

"Maybe. We'll see if Belmont destroys any more equipment. That's about all the excitement we get to see on our end. Have a good night," the Scorn joked as Lucas entered his room.

"Good luck." Lucas smirked. He shut the door to his quarters then it locked automatically. He turned the handle only to realize a display flickered at eye level. "Drill in session, Mr. Anderson. Would you like to page a guard for an escort?"

"No, no," he replied.

"Thank you." The text display acknowledged his voice then turned off. Clearly, the installation was built around much older technology. It wasn't even a holographic display.

Getting in his bed, he was reminded of being back on a naval warship again. The bed was small with an ultra-thin mattress that might as well have been a slab of plywood. He pulled out a small tablet, breathing on it. His condensation unlocked the display, illuminating part of the room with a blue tint.

"Welcome, Lucas Anderson," a pleasant female voice greeted. Lucas' pupils guided the 3D interface as it rotated and closed various applications to reveal his message inbox. He opened the top message, which was from his assistant.

"Mr. Anderson. Just wanted to let you know the asset is fine. All the readings are perfect. We'll see you when you return. Stay warm... if that's even possible!"

"A comfortable bed, that's what isn't possible," Lucas said, shifting around.

Like SolarSystems, the Fifth Column had its secrets. Lucas found things on his expeditions that he wanted to guard closely. So close that even his business partners didn't know about them. Most of it was military related, however, one of his secrets was much different.

So different that it would alter the course of human history forever.

Lucas' role in the Star Rust race seemed specialized to SolarSystems. At first, Dr. Amery saw Lucas as a connected soldier more than an entrepreneur or idealist, but over the years, he began to become more suspicious. Lucas had a first responder position. Amery had no idea what they found in the field, he simply had to take Lucas at his word.

On one of Lucas' very first missions, before he had officially founded his organization, he discovered a fully intact escape pod from the alien craft. Lucas kept the information about what was inside away from SolarSystems and the entire world.

Maintaining SolarSystems as a partner meant keeping a close eye on them. Lucas understood that Amery viewed his organization as nothing more than a bunch of well-equipped treasure hunters, but he couldn't have been more mistaken.

The reality was, Lucas didn't need SolarSystems. He'd held the key to technological advancement for years.

Another reason Lucas kept SolarSystems around was because he needed a behaviorism expert for what he'd found. He had known Keith through the grapevine, and most everyone had great things to say. However, he needed to get in on the ground level with Keith and enter his comfort zone. Lucas needed to be sure.

Keith was perfect for the job, really. He had such a variety of training and skillsets that seemed custom tailored for what Lucas needed. Not to mention his tenacity and devotion to the ECHO project. The ECHO was about as close to alien as it came. But despite that, Lucas had to make sure.

After all, Lucas wanted to hire him for one of the most important jobs the human race had ever known—the first interaction specialist between us and *them*.

***

Several hours later, three Marines headed down to a hanger bay to recover the crippled drone, Icepick. Their mission was to repair his sensor array and use him as a mobile radar. His weapon systems would probably have to wait for repair.

"Still can't believe Icepick survived that avalanche, not to mention made his way back here," the corporal said.

"Yeah. That fucking robot is more of an asset to the Marines than you are," the other corporal joked to his comrade, pushing him in the corridor.

They started to horseplay, wrestling around for a moment until their superior, Sergeant Martin, put a stop to it. "Guys, chill out! You know Belmont has access to all these cameras, so quit it," Sergeant Martin ordered. "You're making life worse than it already is."

"That's pretty damn bad then," one of them joked.

"Shut. Your. Hole," Martin demanded, cutting him down with his eyes.

Sergeant Martin was in command of this squad. He was much more seasoned than the two young Marines. He'd seen three combat tours, but his rank didn't show it. At the very least, he should have been a staff sergeant. He was about average height and build, with thin blond hair and fair skin. He had a birthmark just above the right side of his lip about the size of a half dollar.

Sergeant Martin was the only Marine in Belmont's unit that testified against him for assault charges, and since then Martin's life had been hell. Belmont couldn't get rid of him with a transfer because Martin was one of only three Marines that understood the drone's navigational systems completely.

Since Belmont couldn't transfer Martin, he tortured him by giving him Marines in the unit with the lowest performance marks which affected his statistics. As elite as these Marines were, they still had bad apples that barely scraped by, and Martin got them all.

The two corporals traded obscenities and shoved each other one last time before obeying Martin's order. Up ahead, the long corridor ran into a large hanger. Several vintage Osprey military aircraft were littered about, being stripped for parts it appeared. Looters had also pinched parts before the military reacquired the installation for drone testing.

"Damn, look at all this. There's probably shit in this hanger that would make us rich. Some of these parts are probably worth five years of our salary," the corporal joked.

"Really? Well, how do you reckon you'll get those parts past Garza's inspection when we leave? Not to mention the x-ray scanners when we get back to Camp Lejeune?" Martin pointed out. He stopped in the middle of the hall, waiting for an answer. The corporal was at a loss for words.

"That's right. *Shut* up, Corporal. You ain't gonna *do* shit. Always looking for an easy way out," Martin said, silencing him. The corporal simply snapped away, scratching his chin.

The corporal remained silent while his comrade snickered. "What a dumbass. You're a Marine parts smuggler now?"

"You know, on another note, I wouldn't mind if Garza's inspections were a bit more *personal*, if you know what I mean." The corporal stuck out his tongue.

Martin stopped dead in his tracks. "No, what do you mean?"

"I mean, maybe she could check my boxers next time. I got something hiding in there she might—"

Martin burst toward the Marine, shoving him in the chest and knocking him down. "That woman would *stomp* your ass in five seconds."

"Ahhh, shit—I'd let her." He smiled, slowly picking himself up.

"Get up, you dumb drone. That's some typical sexist bullshit right there. It would be best for you if you started respecting your superiors. When we get done here, you'll be scrubbing the head for the rest of your service." Martin gave the grunt a final kick with the toe of his boot and turned to continue on their path.

They made their way through the hanger, eyeing a vehicle bay door in the corner.

Martin walked over to the bay door, pulling up his holomap. "Okay. Looks like Icepick should be right outside this door."

He pressed the door switch, but initially it didn't open. It seemed to be jammed from either lack of use or the freezing temperature... or a combination of both. He slammed his rifle's stock against the switch and it flashed open.

"See, that's how people did things back then—you'd just smash it," Martin joked.

The motor yanked the door up slowly. The wind exhaled into the hanger, freezing the air. Snowflakes skipped across the concrete surface. They could see Icepick obscured in the distance. He was stopped about fifty meters from the door.

"Did Icepick really just stop *there*? Why is he so far away?" the corporal questioned. The wind howled intensely, swaying the drone's five-foot tall crippled frame back and forth as they looked him over from inside.

"I don't know. His navigation system is up and running, but he's not communicating. Ugh. Send a force order for him to pull inside. Hurry up. This air is *cold*!" Martin ordered in a rushed, annoyed tone.

"I'm already on it." The corporal keyed in the command on his tablet, causing Icepick to lunge forward awkwardly before leveling out his speed, almost as if he was attempting to refuse the order.

"Whoa. Did he just try to negate that order?" Martin said with a confused look on his face.

"Yeah, it's fine. His tracks are probably warped with all that weight being smashed down on him. I mean, he *was* in an avalanche," the corporal said.

"Thanks for the clarification, Corporal. Anytime I need a smartass, it's comforting to know you'll never let me down," Martin said.

As Icepick got closer to the door, they could hear his damaged motor churning. It was normally silent. The sensor array atop his head was dangling by a set of wires, and his guns were mangled beyond recognition.

"All right, he's in. Shut that damn snow blower of a door!" Martin ordered.

The corporal walked over and smashed the door's control just like he was taught. Sure enough, it worked, closing twice as fast as it opened.

"You do have basic cognitive ability. Amazing," Martin joked.

"I thought I was the smartass?" the corporal replied, raising his eyebrows.

The door slammed, instantly silencing the howling wind, like pressing a mute button. All they could hear was Icepick's hybrid motor running.

"Well, the battery powered motor is toast. He's running nothing but diesel," Martin observed.

"Let's shut him down. We can at least get his sensors up and running," the corporal said while scanning over the battered drone.

"Ohhhh wha..."

Suddenly, Martin heard a thud. He panned over to see his corporal lying on the ground, foaming at the mouth. Then, before the other corporal could assess the situation, a jolt rocked him from behind, knocking him out.

"Shit!" Martin raised his rifle, calling in for support. *"This is fire team Alpha. I need immediate—"*

In one motion, his rifle was smacked to the ground violently, his helmet knocked off and flung across the hanger. This ceased communication with his fellow Marines. The large, vacant hanger echoed every sound. He could clearly hear his Marines' response inside the helmet from twenty meters away. "Sergeant Martin? What's going on? *Please respond*!" Garza called out from inside Martin's helmet, far from his reach.

Suddenly, a large talon-like foot appeared, uncloaking just in front of him. Quarter-sized hexagon panels materialized, which then began to take shape and color, unveiling the prototype's true form from bottom to top.

"Oh God."

His talons mashed down on Martin's weapon, crushing it like a toy. The sound echoed across the hanger as Martin stood frozen.

Saven kicked the broken pieces under Martin's feet. Despite all Martin's training, the rallying from his comrades, and the fact this was just a drill—he couldn't focus. None of that mattered. He sat down on the deck and buried his face in his knees like a young child, completely petrified.

Belmont dashed over to the control station and immediately brought up the hanger's camera to see what was happening.

"Oh, whaaaat the hell... Get fire team support down there ASAP! GO!" Belmont ordered. His eyelid quivered while watching the camera. He could feel Martin's terror, even over the fuzzy video feed. The prototype was in full view for the first time.

Saven's posture morphed, appearing very primal and dominating. He towered over Martin, hunching in like a wild animal playing with its prey. His face was inches away from Martin's, basking in his fear, breathing on him. Saven's long metal canine teeth were directly in front of Martin's eyes as he slowly panned across his face. Martin could see saliva streaming from his mouth. He could feel the warm condensation on his skin.

Belmont quickly signaled to Garza to get a team in there ASAP. "GO!"

"What's it doing?" Garza peeked her head up.

"I don't know, but we should use this as an opportunity while it's distracted," Belmont said.

Martin could feel Saven breathing on his face. The stench was terrible, that of rot. He glared up at Saven to show he wasn't afraid, but he had to look away. Saven appeared supernatural, like a demonic wraith. With fangs and glowing green eyes, he was the thing of nightmares. Part machine, part hell-spawn.

"J-J-Just do whatever you're going to do! Go ahead!" Martin begged, closing his eyes and expecting the worst. Belmont watched as the ECHO prototype vanished into the shadows on camera.

"Where'd it go?" Belmont demanded, looking at Garza.

"Sir... I don't... see it," Garza replied.

Martin gritted his teeth and braced for the worst, but it never happened. After several seconds, he opened his eyes to find nothing but his unconscious allies. His eyes were watering, his hands were shaking, and he was covered in a cold sweat. Despite Belmont and his men's distance from Saven, they too had been affected by what they saw.

"Whoa, what the hell was that thing? That's no drone," one of the younger corporals said, getting a quick glimpse of the crowd. His eyes darted away from the rest of the Marines, his heart racing, while his mind attempted to make sense of the anomaly.

"That can't be real. That's not what we're fighting, right?" Someone else gasped.

Belmont turned around. "Go back to your stations! Get away from the screen!"

Many of the Marines walked back slowly with a grim look on their faces. Those who didn't see Saven began asking questions.

"What...what was it? Who got a look at it? I didn't see anything?" a Marine asked.

That was exactly the effect SolarSystems wanted to inflict on the human psyche—The Echo Effect. Fear and confusion so powerful it reverberated through Saven's enemies like shockwaves.

This was training. None of the shots fired were lethal, but you couldn't tell Martin that. He didn't even expect the ECHO prototype to be anywhere near them. None of the sensors picked up anything. It just didn't seem possible.

Chapter Thirteen

Up in the observation booth, Agent Casser had his finger on Saven's kill switch, making sure the war game didn't go overboard. It wasn't likely, the ECHO prototype was programmed to preserve friendly units at all costs, but Casser was ready. Just in case.

"Did anyone else pick up on that?" Casser questioned his team. They were all wide eyed and watching the video feed.

"The Marines' sensors didn't pick up a single thing. Why? Any ideas? Anyone have a theory?" Casser paused, seeming to bask in the puzzled look of his subordinates.

"His proximity to Icepick. Hitching a ride on the drone concealed Saven's electronic signature," Agent Niven confidently answered. By his tone, he knew his answer was correct or a damn good guess.

"Exactly. Genius strategy, actually. Saven literally traveled within ten meters of the other drones on the way back, riding on Icepick, yet nothing suspicious was reported. Our sensors here never picked it up either. Nothing," Casser said.

"Icepick couldn't communicate that something was wrong. He was sent back on forced override orders. I'm not 100% sure Icepick knew anything with his sensors being damaged, but the drone was acting unusual, almost like he was trying to warn the Marines," Niven said.

"That's certainly possible." Casser shrugged, raising his eyebrows.

"That is just...unbelievable. Have you ever seen artificial intelligence do anything this creative?" Agent Niven questioned.

"Who said it was *artificial* intelligence?" Casser posed. "I thought you were checking to see if any encrypted signals were being transmitted from a remote location?"

"Everyone, pay attention to Garza's camera. Listen to what they are talking about, not just the action. She's going down to assess the situation," Casser said.

Two Marine fire teams entered the hanger, fanning out to secure it. Garza walked over to the downed Marines. They were groggy, but recovering. "Get up. You guys are sitting the rest out in the penalty box," Garza ordered.

The downed Marines looked at each other in surprise. "Penalty box, how? What happened?"

"You guys are done. Report to the penalty box for the rest of the drill. We'd be cleaning up your blood if this was real," Garza said, scratching her forehead.

Some young soldier shrugged and shouldered his weapon. "There's really not much they could have done, Staff Sergeant Garza."

"Why do you say that, Corporal?"

"The prototype was invisible, both physically and electronically."

"Hmm," she said suspiciously.

"Clear! Nothing here, Sergeant. It's gone," the Marines sounded off, securing the hanger.

"Sergeant Martin?" Garza said. Her fellow Marine was still sitting on the deck, unresponsive and terrified.

"Sergeant Martin!" Garza yelled. "I know you can hear me. Get up and help your corporal back to the penalty box. You were in charge here. It's the least you can do."

Martin swayed to his feet, glancing at his comrades. His blue eyes were bloodshot and distant. One of the corporals questioned Martin as he assisted them. "What was it? Did you get a good look?"

"Yeah. I saw it. Up close. And you don't wanna see it. It looked like a walking nightmare—" Martin started.

Garza closed the distance explosively, interrupting Martin by shoving her finger in his face and grabbing his collar. "Shut up. No one asked you to come down here and fuck this up, did they? If you say another word about that thing, I'll leave you here with it," Garza threatened.

She was stern with her words but kept her voice down. Maybe she felt there was no need to humiliate the ranking Marine further in front of subordinates.

"I have no idea why it even left you in the game, but you're here, and we'll need you," Garza said.

"Um, thanks, Garza. Can you...let go of my collar?" Martin suggested, looking down at his shirt.

Garza released him.

They had served in combat together back when they were just lance corporals. Garza was given the honor of command Sergeant over Martin, and it created a bit of tension between them. But nothing they couldn't work out. They were friends at one point. Good friends.

Martin's reaction to the prototype was humiliating, considering his experience in real combat. The plan was to come to the Crucible, plow through the opposition and get back to base. He had one simple job, and the whole damn thing fell apart on him.

"Hey, Martin. Look, man, I'm sorry. I shouldn't talk to you like that," Garza said.

"Not after the shit we've been through," Martin said.

Sergeant Martin wasn't due for a blemish on his reputation. Ten years in the Corps and he was just now up for staff sergeant—dishearteningly slow advancement. He'd shown early signs of post-traumatic stress disorder and suicidal tendencies. But after some time, he'd sought regular counseling and was on the road to recovery.

"We got this. I'm telling you guys, it'll slip up sooner or later. This thing can only be sneaky for so long," Garza said, panning around at her men.

Martin raised his eyebrows in disagreement, peering over at her. "I like the confidence. I really do."

"Good. Maybe if you had some of it, you'd have another rocker on your sleeve, *Sergeant*," Garza said.

"Would I, *Staff Sergeant*?" Martin said. He knew that regardless of his efforts, Belmont was keeping him down.

"Maybe, but then you'd have to get rid of that sourpuss attitude," she said.

"So does sourpuss mean *not* Belmont's little bitch?"

"Ha!" Garza smiled. "That's what I like about you, Martin. You get your ass handed to you, but you fire right back."

"Oh, that's what you liked about me all these years?"

"That and the STD above your lip that you call a birthmark," she said as a couple of her Marines busted out in laughter.

"You had to go there with the birthmark, didn't you? You just couldn't resist?" Martin replied. He didn't look happy. It was bad enough being humiliated by the prototype, and now Garza was adding fuel to the fire.

"Staff Sergeant Garza!" A young Marine cupped his hands across the hanger.

"What?"

"Can we go back now? That thing is out here somewhere and our forces are split up," he said.

Garza cocked her head at Martin. "See, it's rubbing off on my Marines now."

"Fuck off, Garza," Martin said, cutting his eyes at her. He wasn't joking either.

"I love you too, Martin."

Martin and the rest of the Marines reentered the command station after dropping off his downed corporals in the penalty box to wait out the rest of the drill. Martin plopped down in one of the operator's chairs, exhausted. Belmont watched his body language like a hawk in front of the young, impressionable Marines. He cut his eyes over at Martin.

Martin instantly started to babble. "I hate to be the bearer of bad news... I do... But you guys are screwed. That thing isn't like anything we've trained for. It's not. I'm telling ya, it's fast, it's smart, and it's going to pick us apart," he said.

Martin paused. He could see Belmont's unsympathetic reaction with his arms crossed. Martin still had the attention of the young Marines. "I didn't even see it. The thing jumped off Icepick and dropped my men before I could even react. We might as well just forfeit and go ho—" Martin stopped mid-sentence, his eyes widened.

Suddenly, Belmont snatched a rifle from the nearest Marine. He shot Martin in the chest with a stun round at close range. The force blew his cap off and spun him around in his chair, knocking him unconscious onto the floor.

"Holy shit," some young corporal mumbled.

The rest of Marines in the control room froze and complete silence ensued. Everyone stared at Martin's body as drool began to stream from his mouth.

Belmont paced for several steps, refusing to make eye contact with anyone. "Clean that fucking infection off my deck... NOW! Before anyone else gets it!" Belmont roared.

Garza hesitated, but signaled two Marines toward Martin's body. "S-Send him down to the penalty box. You heard him," she said.

Two Marines rolled Martin onto a stretcher and carried him off. Belmont stared at Garza for a few seconds.

"Garza," he said.

"Yes, sir," she responded looking at ground. Belmont pointed outside the room. "Come on," he said. She followed close behind as they walked outside the control room. The remaining Marines followed them with their eyes.

"Everybody get on your stations; the drill is still active!" Belmont snapped just before he and Garza exited. He slammed the door behind Garza.

"Now listen... you and I *both* know how this works," he said. He put this hand on the top of the doorframe as she stood up straight at attention.

"Yes, Captain," she replied.

"We've seen this a dozen times. Remember North Korea? If we let one person start that bullshit, we lose. Many of these guys are untested. They don't know what *we* know about combat. You've seen it since you were young. How old were you when you first fired a gun in combat?" Belmont asked.

"Before my first kiss," she replied.

"See. At ease, Staff Sergeant. These guys don't understand that sort of life. They have to fear me more than that… *thing*… whatever the hell it is. I had to make an example of Martin," he gushed. Garza sniffed and jerked her thumb at the Marines through the glass.

Belmont cut her off. "Look, I don't expect you to lead exactly like me, I don't. What I do expect is you to obey without question. You're second in command. I don't won't any hints in your eyes that you disagree. If I can see it, so can they. I have my style and I don't give a shit who disagrees. Matter of fact, you see me questioning how you lead?" Belmont asked.

"No, sir," she said.

"Exactly, some of the shit you do I don't always like, but you get the fucking job done," Belmont said. He focused in on her eyes, pointing sternly at her.

"I understand completely, sir."

"Good."

There was no exception to the rule, friend or foe. When you're out at the Crucible, you're out.

Chapter Fourteen

Back at Keith's station, he awoke to a page from Casser.

"We now have three Marines down. Phase two is in full swing. All non-essential personnel, stay in your designated areas. The prototype and Marine elements are aware of these restricted areas, so stay put," Casser ordered, looking at his people.

"Whoooa!" Keith said, wiping his head and smacking the display's feed. Saven's camera started working. The image was flickering but visible.

"Phase two already?" Keith said.

Lucas entered the room, escorted by one of the guards. "Great news, huh?" Lucas said excitedly.

"Yeah, but I have no idea how Michael made it here undetected," Keith said.

Lucas paused, staring at Keith. "You just called it Michael."

"Well, you know what I mean. Saven... using *Michael's* innovative human mind," Keith recovered.

"I get it," Lucas said, smiling.

"Well, let's watch the show! We have his camera working again. Have a seat," Keith suggested.

Casser focused on Saven's camera for a while.

Oddly, Saven was still in the hanger where Martin's team was attacked. He was watching the Marines from above, waiting in the rafters. He seemed to be assessing their tactics and response time.

After an hour, Saven found a weak spot in the ceiling. He pressed up on it, breaking through to the roof. Normally, he would have used his plasma saber to slice through, but it was disengaged for the drill. He leapt up on top of the roof then looked down as snow fell through the hole he'd just created. He lowered his body, stalking like a cat across the roof.

Snow was falling hard as he looked out into the distance. He could see some of the brute drones surrounding the base. They were looking down below him, unaware of his presence. He skimmed along the side of the roof, looking toward a set of buildings below him.

He jumped off, projecting his shards into a wing formation, gliding to the adjacent building. Considering all the metal, he landed gracefully and with precision. He pressed forward, leaping gaps of fifteen meters between structures. Saven stalked low and moved meticulously across the rooftops to an old office building, clambering through a broken window.

He was moving closer to his final target.

He could hear the classic sound of perimeter defenses ahead. A pulsing audio cue was being emitted, the tick tock of a drone's sensor panning back and forth. He eased around a corner, spotting a small motion detecting drone about a meter tall. It looked like a metallic bullet shaped trash can. Saven strolled right out in front of the stationary robot and stood there. The drone whipped toward him, alerting the Marines of his location.

"That looked... intentional," Lucas said, watching the video feed.

"Oh, no doubt. He clearly saw that drone before walking in front of it," Keith noted.

"I'd think so."

"What's he doing now?" Lucas asked.

Saven kneeled down in front of the detection drone and stared at it. He pushed it with his claws as it rocked back and forth. He jumped around it like a cat playing with its food. It rolled down the hall as he chased it, smacking it around as it clanked against the walls.

"Really?" Lucas smirked.

"Yeah. That's just what he does from time to time. Saven's genetic fusion from the UNIMEL affects his behavior in odd ways. Jaguars are lethal predators, but as you can see, they're still cats," Keith said smiling. He shrugged his shoulders as Lucas shook his head side to side.

The drone's alarm blared louder. This seemed to annoy Saven. He ran it down, swatting it into the air as its red lights and sirens echoed off the walls. He shot it midflight with a stun round and it crashed to the floor, pieces of metal exploded everywhere. Electricity shot out of the drone's front sensor as it shook violently.

"Looks like he's making a whole lotta noise down there," Lucas joked.

"Yeah, that's about as intentional as it gets, but at least it looks like he's having fun," Keith said.

Saven stopped after destroying the drone, peering toward the Marine's station and waiting. He activated his cloak, vanishing into the silvery surfaces like a camouflaged predator.

"Here we go!" Casser said, looking around the control room and rubbing his hands together. He panned over toward Belmont's cameras.

Belmont immediately ordered fire teams to the location. "Fire team Blue, I'll need a situational report as soon as you get down there," Captain Belmont ordered.

The Marines jumped to the challenge.

"Staff Sergeant Garza, *you* lead them this time," Belmont said confidently.

"Locked, cocked and ready to rock, sir!" She raised her weapon. Garza led out in front, exiting the control room and rushing toward the prototype.

The Marines stacked up in formation outside the hall where Saven was spotted, slowly clearing it.

"This place is completely abandoned, Sergeant."

"Sir, we don't have anything down here, and it was supposedly *just* here," Garza responded.

Back at the station, Belmont had his command team scroll through the sensors and cameras for any signs of the prototype.

"Keep searching. He's there," Belmont ordered.

Sweat was dripping down Garza's forehead. As cold as it was outside, she was feeling the heat where she was. She knew the prototype only had two routes that led to Belmont, and her team was the only defense for one of them.

"Ah, really? Well, there it goes. It cut the power," Garza said. "Switching to night vision."

As soon as the light sensor dropped below a certain reading, the Marine's helmets automatically extended a holographic visor over their eyes. The visor lit up the dark room as if it was daylight while detecting movement better than the human eye.

"Cutting the power? That's old-school." One of the blue team corporals laughed. His head was shaking while he said it, but maybe humor helped him deal with the situation.

"It has to know we have night vision. That's nearly a hundred-year-old technology," another Marine responded.

"Shut up. Of course it knows we have night vision, it's attempting to make us feel reliant on technology, which is exactly what *it* represents… a changing of the guard," Garza said.

Blue team crept around the winding installation. Covering every possible angle, they glided through a set of abandoned offices and found a ceiling fan still slowing after the power cut. The team lead peered around the cabinets and desks, hunting for any signs of activity.

The dust in the room was over an inch thick. Tablets and computers were left behind in the scramble to evacuate. To a horror fan, the scene looked like something out of zombie film. These people left everything in a panic.

And what a panic it must have been. North Korea lobbed tactical nuclear weapons only seventy-five miles from this very location. The fear of imminent fallout must have been terrifying.

One corporal happened to look out the window into the light snowfall. "What the hell? The drones…look at 'em!"

Oddly, the remaining drones just surrounded that part of the building, pointing their guns toward them as if they knew something was there, but it was too late. The drones weren't allowed to participate in phase two.

"They're just… looking at us," another corporal said.

One of the Marines yelled from the back of the formation. "Yeah, well, they can't help us now. They should have done their damn jobs and we wouldn't be dealing with this."

Someone whispered in the eerie silence. "I'm not gonna lie, this whole thing is creeping me the fuck out."

"Cut the chatter and push forward. It could have only gone one direction. Let's show it what we're about and go home," Garza ordered.

Two of the Marines looked toward one another after Garza's comment, assessing each other's reaction. Neither appeared confident, but they didn't dare respond and show a lack of sureness either. They were Marines. Confidence was the uniform of the day, *every* day.

Luckily, Garza fit the bill, inside and out. "You weak minded new guys are gonna let this thing get inside your heads? Really? A drone? Listen, it took out a couple of brutes with an avalanche. That's cute. It took out Martin's guys when they weren't paying attention. Wow. Let's see how it deals with devil dogs sniffing for its ass."

"This is our turf, and this is what we do!" Garza barked with confidence.

"Ooo-Rah!" The corporals bellowed out in unison.

Belmont and the few operators left could hear Garza's speech. "That's what I'm talking about, people! That's a real Marine with confidence right there," Belmont said, looking around at his Marines. "Let that be an example."

Garza ordered her men to push forward. They continued on in formation, pushing toward a slightly ajar door into some type of huge lab. The lead corporal eased the door open, but it creaked loudly the slower he pressed it.

Wham! Garza ran up and slammed it open. "I don't think it matters, does it?" she said, smirking.

"Whhaaat the hell is this place?" one of the lance corporals whispered.

"I didn't get to see this before. We never had a prototype even make it to the installation phase, so we never got to explore. Remember trigger discipline, folks. Short, controlled bursts," Garza said.

They made their way into a large room with high ceilings. The walls, floor, and ceiling appeared to be an aluminum alloy. Around the outer wall were metallic tables with lab microscopes and computers.

In the middle of the room, dozens of massive, elevated glass containers stood evenly throughout the room. They looked like huge fish tanks of some sort. Backup emergency green lights highlighted the interiors of the tanks. Some of them weren't working while others strobed and flickered.

At some point, the tanks contained something, but the contents had been removed a long time ago. The containers were grimy, many still full of water, and each had a coat of dark green residue on the top layer.

The tanks had vital sign gauges, so whatever they kept inside them was definitely alive.

"Ahhh, what the hell.... What did they keep in here? That smell, ugh." Garza coughed. "It smells like sewage."

"Looks like they were experimenting with bioweapons of some sort," one the Marines mentioned.

"Great, so not only were they dealing with fallout warnings, it looks like these *things* got loose?" Garza noticed.

The Marines split into two groups inside the room, checking every inch of it. Most had to pinch their noses, and their mouths were curled downward in displeasure at the hideous odor.

"Anyone thirsty?" Garza said. "Go ahead and fill your canteens with this slime and show me how much of a man you *really* are." She peered into one of the tanks.

"I'm good, Staff Sergeant," someone said.

"Whoa!"

The lights came back on and the Marines' visors retracted back into their helmets. "Well, that didn't last long," Garza said. The light transition lasted only a split second, but it was just enough of a diversion.

Suddenly, a blurred figure darted right between the Marines' formation. The movement startled them and they reacted, opening fire as the form disappeared into the room they'd just exited. The sound of glass shattering and gunfire was amplified in the metallic room.

"I think I hit it!" One of the Marines cheered. Their stun rounds shattered several of the massive glass containers, spilling hundreds of gallons of slimy water into the room and filling it ankle high.

Two Marines were struck in the crossfire by friendly rounds, knocking them unconscious.

"I've got...two down. I say again, two Marines down from friendly fire. Watch your targets!" Garza ground her teeth.

"Contact! Over there!" Garza searched around for her explosives expert. "Put an EMP in that room! Now!"

The tech Marine fumbled around for a second before grabbing a grapefruit-sized device out of his satchel. The modified EMP grenade was designed to electronically scramble almost any tech device.

The Marine tossed the grenade toward the door. The trajectory was perfect as the Marine's eyes followed the EMP just as it was going through the door. Then wham! Shut.

The door slammed, knocking the EMP down as it splashed into the water.

"Get in the—" Garza started to yell for everyone to jump in the elevated tanks, but it was too late. The EMP detonated in the water, frying the Marine's communications and weapon systems temporarily. Some of the Marines fell down trying to make quick movements to avoid the blast. But with their full gear, it was nearly impossible.

"Ohhhh! No no no!" Belmont yelled.

Lucas and Keith watched Saven's video feed as he casually reentered the room.

"It's like we're watching a horror flick, except we want the monster to win." Lucas smiled excitedly.

Keith didn't say a word. His eyes were glued to the tube.

"Hey!" Lucas said, trying to get Keith's attention.

"Click... Click... Click..." The Marines pulled their weapon's triggers, but nothing happened. Their wet armor had sensory circuitry to detect impacts for the drill, which connected to their weapons. The EMP blast had traveled up their armor, disabling weapons.

Saven entered the room slowly, almost casually, shooting the Marines execution style as some tried to stand up. Most of them were shot point blank in the face. He stepped over their bodies as he moved forward.

"No! Don't..." a corporal begged, putting his hands up as Saven shot him while he attempted to stand up.

The pulsing sound of the stun round reverberated through the room with each blast. Garza could hear a shot followed by a splash as each Marine fell into the water.

Garza hid inside one of the elevated containers, unaffected by the EMP blast. She watched through the shattered glass as the prototype evened the odds, taking one Marine out after another. They were helpless. Garza scrambled around, but couldn't find her weapon. She knew if it didn't hit the water, she might still have a chance.

Garza spun around in the container and saw her gun dangling by the shoulder strap on a shard of glass, safe from the water's electric zap. Garza needed to figure out something—fast. The prototype had finished every Marine in the room, except her.

Casser watched on from Saven's perspective. His sensors were directing him toward a homing beacon in the room—the sound of a single fluttering heart rate. Saven's head cocked sideways as he headed toward the signal.

Garza slowly reached down and grabbed her weapon. She could see the ECHO's blurred reflection in the opposite container's glass. It was slowly skulking through the soiled waters toward her.

"Oh god!"

"Sir?" One of the corporals questioned Belmont as they watched the video feed back at the control station. "Should we help her?"

"There's nothing we can do," Belmont said, widening his eyes. "By the time we get down there, it'll be over."

Watching Belmont's second in command fight for her simulated life looked real to Casser. It looked real to everyone. Keith was nearly pulling out his hair. Both he and Lucas were standing up, silently watching Saven's every move.

All eyes were on Garza. *Do or die, semper fi.*

Garza could see the invisible form gingerly and silently creeping towards her, creating ripples in the water. She'd moved down to the ground level, leaning up against the container. The prototype's demeanor was different. Previously, it moved incredibly fast, but it was moving slowly and with confidence, one step at a time.

"Garza, it's Belmont. If you can hear me, take the shot. It's just standing there. I say again, *take* the shot! It doesn't know your weapon is functional!"

Against her better judgment, Garza followed the order to be aggressive. She quickly snatched the weapon up into firing position. In the reflection, she saw a pair of green eyes snap toward her position. She turned and fired on the ECHO, and then rolled behind another container.

"Shit!"

Then, there was silence. She waited for any sound that might give away Saven's position, but there was nothing. Garza continued to use the container's reflection to look for any signs of its location.

"Where's it at, people? Use the cameras from our downed Marines! They are working again. Anyone see it? Talk to me!" Belmont demanded.

Garza scanned the room, noticing a circle of water that looked unnatural. Ripples pinged around it.

She immediately fired just short of the anomaly. The splash covered the ECHO's invisible form, revealing his position.

"Sssssssssssssssssssssssssssssshhhhhhhhhhhh!" Strangely, the ECHO hissed like a cobra as water rolled down its face, dripping off his massive fangs. Saven spewed water out toward Garza.

Casser jumped back in his seat.

"Sir, you all right?" Niven smiled.

"Yeah, yeah, that sound was a bit louder than I expected."

A surge of energy erupted from the Saven's position, slinging water everywhere as the ECHO dashed away in a blur. Garza scoped in and fired, but it seemed the prototype could anticipate her shots, zig zagging back and forth.

After every shot, Belmont glanced at the prototype's life bar on the holographic display. All it took was one shot and Garza could end it.

"Go, *dammit*! You got 'em!" A Marine yelped as they all huddled around Belmont's monitor, watching the video feed from Garza's shoulder-mounted camera. It was frightening. The camera bobbed up and down as she panted, peering around the container for the prototype.

Garza stopped.

One of her unconscious Marines slumped face down in the water.

"Drill, cease fire. Marine in danger!" Garza waved to the camera and pointed, trying to get Casser's attention.

Before Agent Casser could even respond, Saven lifted the Marine's head out of the water, flipping him over on his back against the wall. The man started coughing, spitting up water. He was still unconscious, but alive.

Garza drew her gun down on the ECHO as he helped her Marine. She pulled the trigger in slightly, but not enough to fire. "H-He all right?"

Casser's pen fell out of his mouth just as he was about to pause the drill. "He just put himself at risk to save that Marine." Casser chuckled.

"The drill has been suspended. All hands await further instruction before proceeding," Casser ordered over the loudspeaker. He turned to view the vitals holochart that depicted the Marine in question.

LANCE CORPORAL HOLLEN STEWART – STATUS - UNCONSCIOUS - STABLE

"He's fine. Okay, let's resume the drill and we'll send a medical unit down there immediately afterward," Casser said, pressing the intercom button.

"Wait," Niven interjected.

"What, Niven?"

"Agent Casser, sir. Can we have a word alone?" Niven requested.

"Uh sure," Casser said, getting up from his chair. He followed Niven outside of the room while the other agents trailed them with their eyes.

"You really think what we just witnessed was artificial intelligence?" Niven whispered, arms crossed, looking through the glass back into their control room.

"That or someone is remotely controlling this prototype. Still no evidence that supports that?"

"None."

"There is another option for this behavior," Casser said suspiciously.

"Cybernetics," Niven immediately fired back.

"I don't even want to go down that road. You're talking about a media field day—no way to hide it if we press it," Casser said.

"Not only that, the official guidelines don't have regulations in place for cyborgs. It was strangely omitted. I just combed the entire thing after I realized that this was a possibility," Niven replied.

"There was nothing strange about it."

"So, you're saying someone altered the rules?"

"No, Agent Niven. The objective of the Crucible has always been about creating a prototype that was completely self-sufficient *and* efficient."

"So you're telling me *our* government wouldn't mind the concept of cyborgs imbedded within the ranks of our military servicemen?"

Casser looked right at Niven, pausing for a moment before answering. "No. If it gets the job done, no modern politician gives a damn how *sci fi* the premise is. It's more about keeping it out of the public view."

Niven didn't look convinced.

"Just keep your mouth shut about it, Niven. Nothing good will come from this revelation, if it's even true," Casser concluded.

"Um. Understood, sir. I just—"

"Niven, I understand you're new. I get that. The longer you do this job, the more stuff you'll see, and you can't stop it. All we can do is follow the rules. Now, do our rules state anything about Cyborgs?" Casser posed.

"No."

"No, then," Casser said, pointing at Niven's chest. "If you want to be a politician later, then by all means, go try and be a hero there." Casser smiled. "I'll even vote for ya."

Niven looked down at his feet before looking back up. He shook his head in agreement. Casser patted him on the shoulder. "Now, let's go do *our* job."

The agents stormed back into the room and turned their attention to the Marine control room. Belmont's reaction appeared wide-eyed, but he was focused on prepping Garza, like a coach readying his player during a short timeout. "Get ready. Don't let that thing distract you,

Garza. I'm telling you, our cameras show what looks like the enemy at your three o'clock."

"Roger that, sir," Garza said as she looked over her weapon. Her voice was full of forced confidence.

Keith and Lucas looked at one another without a word. The contrast between Saven's methodically murderous mindset in the drill and assumed compassion here was staggering.

"Why are we waiting? That corporal is breathing. I can see it plain as day," Lucas asked.

"Oh my. Hold your horses people. A two-minute break and everyone is freaking out," Casser said as he listened in on Lucas.

"Ladies and gentlemen, prototype and Marines. Ahem. Corporal Stewart is fine," Casser ordered over the loudspeaker. "We will resume the drill on my countdown from ten. Everyone get ready..." Casser instructed. He scanned across his control room briefly, meeting eyes with his subordinates.

"10"

"Come on, Saven!" Keith scurried to his feet.

"9"

"8"

Suddenly, Saven let out a deafening roar that echoed off the walls. The sound shattered the remaining glass and woke up a few Marines that were unconscious. Garza shut her eyes, holding her weapon tight. She hunched closer to the metal container as if she was taking shelter from an approaching storm.

"7"

"No fear, Garza! Do or die, semper fi!" Belmont attempted to yell over Saven's roar. The remaining Marines chimed in over her mic, rallying her.

"6"

"Marines, if you're waking up now, don't move! You are out of the drill!" Belmont ordered.

"5"

"Do or die, semper fi!" the Marines continued, standing to their feet.

"4"

"3"

"2"

"Just one more here Michael, then to Belmont!" Keith yelled, interlocking his fingers behind his head. Lucas glanced over at him, squinting his eyes at Keith.

"1"

"Play ball!" Casser whooped over the loudspeaker in umpire fashion. Garza didn't waste any time getting the jump. She immediately shot at Saven as he darted around the room.

Garza fired aggressively. She could see him better while he was evading, but he was more difficult to fire at. He darted from container to container, encroaching on her position. He was like a rocket fueled boat streaking through the water as it splashed up a wake that reached the ceiling.

"Shit, he's coming in fast!" Lucas observed.

Garza stood up, exposing herself to sight in a shot. She pushed her weapon near the point of overheating. "Shit!"

She let up on the trigger just before the critical point. If the weapon expended too much heat, it would jam.

"One shot. That's all we need!" Belmont yelled.

"Whoa, she's getting mighty close," Lucas said as energy projectiles flashed by Saven's camera.

Saven was forced to jump straight up to avoid Garza's rapid fire assault. He thrust his claws into the high ceiling, suspending himself for a brief moment before he dropped back down.

As he fell, Garza anticipated it, firing ahead where he would naturally land. Saven twisted his body in mid-flight, facing her, prone in midair. He flared out his wings, slowing his fall for a split second. Her shots zipped just underneath him, missing him by inches as he retracted his wings. He landed then retreated behind cover.

"What? That's not possible!" Garza fired, moving toward him to the next row of containers. He was completely visible for a moment when he used his wings, sacrificing camouflage.

"I see it!"

Saven weaved back and forth, closing the distance completely. He was just on the other side of the same container as Garza. They were back to back. Only a couple of meters of aluminum separated them.

"See, it's what Sergeant Martin said about how fast it is," one of the operators in Belmont's control room commented.

"What did you just say?" Belmont snapped around.

"Oh…nothing, sir."

Belmont saw how close the ECHO was on his camera feed. "Garza, it's just around the corner! It's right there!" He smashed his fist into the desk.

The ECHO eased around the side of the container. Garza knew he was there, thanks to Belmont. She unloaded her weapon in the water, trying to land that single victory shot. "Ahhhh!" She furiously fired, yelling as she fought for her simulated life, fighting for her unit's reputation.

The weapon started to give off a warning sound before overheating, but Garza's nerves got the best of her. She pushed it past the limit.

Shoof shoof shoof shoof shoo sho sho

The weapon's sound frequency changed, jamming up. Garza looked down at her weapon as steam poured into her face then back up. Her face instantly changed from intensity to a casual smirk.

"Well, I guess that's it," Garza said to herself, looking at her useless weapon.

"No! No! Don't!" Belmont lunched forward.

Saven rounded the corner, kicking up a stream of soiled water into her eyes. It burned.

"Aaarrghhhh!"

Garza dropped her weapon in her lap, rubbing her eyes. Saven snatched up her rifle, waiting several seconds for it to cool down and for her to open her eyes. When she did, he shot her in the chest with her own gun. The blast knocked her against the container as she slumped over unconscious.

"Yeaaaah!" Keith high-fived Lucas.

Saven dropped Garza's weapon in the water, turning toward the room's camera. Saven must have known Belmont could see him. He stared into the lens for a moment, flashing his green eyes and disappearing like a ghost.

"See that? That's purely psychological. Drones don't do that," Niven said, standing up.

"Get me proof," Agent Casser replied.

"Nooooooo! Damnit!" Belmont pounded the table with his fist several times. He picked up a chair and tossed it into the bulletproof glass. It flexed from the impact and the chair spun wildly across the floor.

"Whoa!" Keith turned toward the racket. Keith just stood in front of the screen, shaking his head. "That was close."

"I can't lie. That was pure entertainment," Lucas said.

"Well, I'm glad you think so. Here I am with my career on the line and you're over there like it's a night at the movies. You need me to make you some popcorn? Maybe a soda?" Keith joked.

"That'd be nice, actually. But people don't scream as much as you do at the real movies, so if you could keep it down, I'd appreciate it." Lucas smiled.

"You could at least *pretend* you're stressed—that'd help," Keith said, pacing the room.

Lucas raised an eyebrow.

"That's right. I forgot I'm talking to a Navy SEAL commander here. There probably isn't much that *does* stress you out at this point," Keith said.

"Not having popcorn during all that was pretty stressful," Lucas replied.

"Ha! I have to give ol' Garza credit though," Keith said.

"That's an understatement. I wouldn't think twice about sending her through SEAL training. I'm not saying she would make it, but I've worked with a lot of military personnel and she's elite, no doubt."

"You did notice Saven wasn't shooting *back* at her, right?" Keith said.

"Yeah, what's that about, anyway?"

"Well, we're talking about it so you'd imagine the Marines are too," Keith said.

"Psychological tactics again," Lucas said, rolling his eyes. "He could have ended it much faster if he would have shot at her."

"Right now, I bet Belmont is wondering how he's being steamrolled by a prototype that doesn't even need his own weapon," Keith said.

"I doubt that. He's probably wondering what he's going to   break   next."

Chapter Fifteen

After tossing the chair, Belmont buried his face in his hands. He knew he had to do something drastic.

He was alone with only a handful of inexperienced Marines. All of them were technical support and probably hadn't fired their weapons in weeks. He was in uncharted territory. Not a single experimental drone had progressed into phase two in nineteen years of the Crucible.

Not only that, but he'd lost his best leader and probably best shooter in the entire unit, Staff Sergeant Garza.

There was only silence in the Marine control room as the young corporals looked toward Belmont for leadership. After a couple minutes, he pulled his face out of his hands. He stood up and met all their eyes with a vacant, yet intense face.

"Stay put until I get back," Belmont said in a low voice, walking out of the room. He marched down the hall toward Keith's control room. He could hear himself breathing heavily as he passed Keith's window. Keith was inside, laughing with Lucas. This angered Belmont, but he kept his cool.

It appeared that Lucas had seen enough for the day and was leaving. Lucas shut the door, telling Keith goodbye. Lucas stood there for a moment, as if he could feel Belmont beside him, staring.

"Captain?" Lucas said. He seemed surprised to see Belmont on that side of the hall. It wasn't common for Marines to leave their own during the Crucible.

"Lucas. Just heading over to discuss a few technical hiccups I'm having with Keith. Wondering if he's experiencing the same," Belmont said, changing his appearance to a more professional manner.

"The drill is still live, isn't it?" Lucas asked.

"Yeah. It'll just take a second though."

"Oh okay. You mean the camera feed hiccups?" Lucas smiled.

"Um, yeah, yeah. You guys too, huh?" Belmont crossed his arms.

"Saven's camera has been quirky the whole drill," Lucas noted. "I'll let you guys work it out. I've got some things to handle on my end."

"See ya tomorrow then," Belmont said. He knew that his visit had nothing to do with technical hiccups, but he played right into it.

Keith noticed Belmont just outside the door, talking to Lucas. They made eye contact through the glass. Keith stood up, confused by Belmont's decision to come over.

"Keith," Belmont greeted him, turning his back and closing the door behind him. He paused awkwardly for a moment.

"Well, Captain, didn't expect to see you here. What's going on? The drill is still live, you know?" Keith said.

"Yeah, yeah. I know. My Marines' camera feeds have been quirky. Have you remedied your issues?" Belmont asked in a low voice. He looked out in the hall to see if Lucas had rounded the corner back to his quarters.

"Um, yeah, for the most part," Keith said, shutting down his monitors. Belmont looked up to the corner wall. There was an old security camera positioned above Keith, the same camera Agent Casser used to monitor the rooms.

"Maybe you could give me some pointers," Belmont said.

"Hmmm, well, yeah, but why are you coming over *now*?" Keith questioned suspiciously, raising his eyebrows.

"What do you mean?"

"Well, all of your tactical Marines with camera feeds are in the penalty box. You only have drone operators remaining," Keith said, raising an eyebrow and staring at Belmont.

Belmont slowly inched toward Keith. He dropped his posed face, revealing one of desperation and anger. Keith's eyes widened as he took a step back.

"Captain, I'm going to have to ask you to leave."

Belmont lunged at Keith, outside the view of protection the camera provided. He grabbed Keith around the throat, picking him up off the floor with ease and holding him at eye level.

It appeared that Keith tried to move into view of the camera, but Belmont's arm reach and power were too great. He outweighed Keith by over 100lbs.

"You little shit," Belmont said furiously. He kept his voice just low enough to not be overheard.

"W-What?"

Belmont got in Keith's face. "That's no fucking drone...*is it?*"

"I-I-I can't breathe..." Keith pleaded. He struggled, attempting to pull down on Belmont's hands, but they didn't move.

"Answer the question! That's no drone, is it?" Belmont demanded. "You wanna fuck with my career? Huh? Embarrass the Marines?" He tightened his grip.

Keith's face started to turn purple, but surprisingly, he smiled. Initially, Belmont thought he was crazy, Keith seemed to invite pain or perhaps death upon himself, but this began to enraged Belmont. He took the smile as taunting.

"Oh, you don't think I will? You think—" Suddenly, the door exploded open, breaking off the top hinge. Saven rocketed into the room like a missile, smashing Belmont with his metallic forearm right in the chest. The impact was tremendous. It knocked Belmont into the air halfway across the room. He landed on top of a desk then rolled off, face down in front of Agent Casser's view.

"Aaaaaaaarggghhhhh!" Belmont groaned.

Keith's leg buckled as he gasped for air. The 300 pound Belmont was hurled off him like a small child.

"Whoa. Whoa. We've got something here on camera six!" Casser said as his agents huddled around him.

Saven rolled Belmont over onto his back with his foot as the captain moaned in pain. The impact had knocked the breath out of him. Saven extended his rifle, pointing it at Belmont's head.

Belmont started to lean up, but when he did, Saven shot him in the face with a stun round without hesitation.

After a few moments, Belmont awakened groaning from the pain. Saven's green eyes gazed down on him in defeat. Keith had pressed his back against the wall, his hands out beside his hips, bracing himself as far away from the action as the wall would allow.

"Oh my god!" Keith yelled, holding his throat and coughing. Saven tossed his rifle at Keith, nodding slowly. Keith awkwardly caught the rifle, trying to catch his breath.

Casser's voice came over the loudspeaker within a few seconds. "AHEM. Gentlemen, we have a winner..."

Belmont forced himself to move around, holding his head as he regained consciousness. He looked over at

Saven first, shaking his head in confusion. Agent Casser and company strolled into the room.

Belmont stood up, and everyone was staring at him. Lucas even had time to hurry down for a peek through the glass in the hall. Belmont looked right at Saven for a split second before turning toward Casser.

"Ughhh." Belmont sighed.

"We were in the control room. I was out of bounds… The drill isn't over," Belmont said under his breath.

"Hmmm, well, where exactly *is* out of bounds for choking a man?" Casser posed.

"He's cheating. That prototype isn't artificial intelligence. That's why I came down here to straighten this out," Belmont said, raising his voice slightly.

"Instead of coming to me and my staff, you decided you could choke out Keith? Well, what did your investigation yield, exactly? If Saven isn't artificial intelligence, then what is he?" Casser demanded.

"I think it's being controlled remotely by a human operator off station," Belmont said, unsure of himself. He looked toward the ground.

"And what evidence do you have?" Casser questioned.

"I'd need some time to prove—" Belmont said under his breath.

"Captain Belmont, there are no signals to or from this installation. My crew has the most advanced sensors in place to ensure this. I can assure you that suspicion is incorrect."

"You're making a huge mistake, Casser," Belmont said, sternly looking at him.

"Am I? You just attacked a military contracted civilian during a war game, Captain Belmont. All I have to do is press a button and your superiors will get video footage." Casser pointed at him. "If you threaten me again, you're done."

"What footage? There's no evidence I did anything," Belmont said. He knew he was careful not to assault Keith within the camera's limited perspective.

Casser stepped in close to Belmont. "You forgot about a camera," Casser said, smiling. He pointed toward Saven's chest to a circular object. "We've got all we need right here."

Belmont rolled his eyes, looking at the ceiling and cursing under his breath. He shook his head in submission. "DAMNIT!"

"Keith Sanders, I want to congratulate you and your team. This is quite the accomplishment. Washington will be pleased to hear about your success." Agent Casser smiled with his hands crossed low in front of him.

"Understand that I will prove my theory is correct. There's no way a drone came in and did this to all my men," Belmont argued.

"Seems to me, no matter what it is, it shouldn't be able to pick apart the most skilled operators the US military has to offer. It was twenty-two Marines and various drones against a single prototype," Casser pointed out. "You can't even give it credit for that?"

"You said it yourself, Belmont. You were upset we only had one drone to test this year," Keith said.

Belmont cut his eyes up at him.

"Dr. Sanders, do you require any medical attention? I apologize for not asking that first, Keith," Casser questioned.

"No. I'm good, thank you," Keith said.

"Ah, very well. Gentlemen, the days of sending human Special Forces troops into dangerous territory could be one step closer to being over. This could save many American lives, gentlemen," Casser continued. "Captain Belmont...we'll be in touch with your superiors soon. I'm sure they'll want to debrief on this evolution in its entirety. We appreciate you and your men's participation," Casser explained.

"I've got nothing else to say to any of you," Belmont said, getting to his feet. "Out of my way." Storming out of the room, he brushed up against Niven's shoulder. Casser's men followed the brutish Marine with their eyes.

Lucas threw both hands around Keith's shoulders. "I know you told *him* you're ok, but—"

"No, I'm good." Keith said. Lucas peered over at Saven in the corner of the room. He was moving around erratically, with short, jerky movements.

"Hey, why's he moving like that?" Lucas asked.

"That's excitement but..."

"He looks like he wants, something." Lucas observed. Saven moved closer to Keith, smacking his hand against the wall violently several times. Brick began chipping away from the surface, flinging chucks across the room and filling the air with smoke and debris.

"What the hell! Keith?! What's he want? Do something!" Lucas demanded, backing away. Suddenly, Saven collapsed to the floor, his metallic exoskeleton crumbled awkwardly. Keith held up his thumb sized remote shutdown. "He just got a little too excited," Keith said casually. He stared out into the distance a million miles away.

"A *little* too excited? Does he not like white colored bricks? Did you promise him something if we won? What?" Lucas asked, pulling his hair back. They had no idea what Amery had done.

"What? No. He has no ambition other than to complete orders."

"That scared the shit outta me. Look at that wall, he took half of it down!" Lucas said.

"I don't think he meant anything by it, he could have killed us if he wanted."

"Well, a heart attack can be fatal, Keith." Lucas said holding his chest.

"It's fine. I'll get some people up here for transport. He won't remember any of this." Keith said.

"You might not either. You're in shock." Lucas observed.

"I need to rest."

"All right come here, gimme your arm. I'll get you to your quarters."

The drill was over. For the first time, the U.S. Marines were defeated at their own game. After successfully winning the Crucible, Saven would soon be in active combat status. He was now capable of being deployed in place of Special Forces teams. The government contract negotiations could start.

Ten hours later, Agent Casser and his men were the first to leave. Keith and Lucas ordered their men to prepare their equipment to head back to the mainland, as did Belmont. The bright morning sun shined in on the concrete surface, blinding to all those around. However, in the distance, heavy snow threatened.

"I still can't believe it," Lucas said, shaking his head as he watched the Marines load their equipment.

"Honestly, I'm surprised it took so long. I felt like Saven was holding back," Keith replied, smiling.

"You cocky son of a bitch." Lucas laughed. "I'm guessing Amery will want me to stay onboard as a partner? For a little while, anyway."

"I'd think so. Yeah," Keith said.

Lucas dropped his head, raising his eyebrows.

"What?" Keith said.

"I have to be honest with you about something, and I know I can trust you not to say anything," Lucas said, biting his lip.

"Absolutely. Go ahead. Shoot."

"Me being here... Well, it has nothing to do with our partnership. I mean, I wouldn't mind keeping it for certain reasons, but not for income," Lucas said.

"Well, then why are you here?" Keith asked, furrowing his eyebrows downward curiously.

"I've heard, for a long while, you are the best at what you do. It's evident after what I've seen here. The way you poured yourself into this project is unbelievable, frankly. You stuck with this program for years, even while you were losing."

"Thanks, but I'm not following."

"I came here to offer you a job. I came to see in person if you were the right man for the job."

"What? You're trying to hire me out from underneath your business partner? Ha! I knew you were a SEAL, but damn, that's cutthroat." Keith laughed, folding some cables up into a metal suitcase.

"Business is business, but this goes beyond all the trivial stuff, Keith. I can't really get into specifics here, but you'll have the chance to work for a company trying to make a positive difference," Lucas said with a serious face.

Keith laughed. "Positive?"

"I know you've been knee deep in the ECHO project, but have you *really* thought about what Saven is designed for? I mean, think about the level of unaccountability that thing offers with its capabilities. He can get in and out behind enemy lines without anyone seeing anything," Lucas posed.

"North Korea is still a threat," Keith replied. "How is defending our nation not positive?"

"I get that. There's no doubt, now that Saven has plowed through the Crucible, he will probably get the opportunity to defend his country, again. That's admirable."

"Then how admirable must we be, Lucas? Apparently, that isn't enough."

"Stop. I'm not judging *you*. I'm not. I want you on my side. I just… Well, I just see you as part of a team that's looking to advance mankind, not continue the same vicious cycle."

"Are you going to stop talking in circles and give it to me straight?" Keith asked.

"Not now. I just ask that you think deeply about my character and Amery's. That's really what it comes down to. I want you to think hard about the ECHO project, think about what SolarSystems was willing to sacrifice to gain an edge here with this program," Lucas explained.

Keith looked away. He understood the moral implications of the ECHO unit, but he wasn't in his right mind when Amery dumped the project on him.

"But listen, when I see you, I see someone who stands out from all that. You don't fit in with those guys. I see a man that understands dedication and has tremendous skill. I see an honest man. I see a man that I want on my side. I can't make it any simpler than that," Lucas said.

Those words seemed more genuine to Keith than anything he could remember hearing in recent events.

Keith looked down at the ground then back up at Lucas. "I appreciate that, I do. I'm not able to make a decision now, but—"

"That's all I'm asking. Just consider my offer," Lucas said, smiling and patting Keith on the back.

Keith shook his head in agreement, but in the back of his mind, he knew he couldn't leave Saven.

Suddenly, Belmont interrupted them. "We're outta here." He extended his hand toward Lucas.

"Lucas." Belmont made eye contact, but only briefly before looking away.

Lucas stared through Belmont. His eyes were vacant, no emotion, refusing to shake his hand while looking up at the towering Marine. Lucas appeared completely confident, not intimidated in the slightest.

Belmont scoffed at Lucas, turning around quickly and shaking his head. "Every Marine on the bird now or your ass gets left here!" Belmont ordered. He looked back at Lucas briefly then over at Keith. He held his stare for a few seconds, squinting his eyes slightly before turning around.

"Move it. Assholes and elbows, people!" He pointed at the jet before boarding.

"He seems rather positive, considering," Keith said, tucking his weapon away. "I'm crushed I didn't get a handshake though. Hurts my feelings, really." Keith stuck out his bottom lip before smiling.

"Your hand would probably be crushed if he shook it." Lucas smiled.

"Better than my throat," Keith said, touching the bruised skin around his neck.

For the first time in a long while, Keith felt a sense of accomplishment, a sense of victory. He'd worked long hours on the ECHO project, and to see it come into its own was like watching a child grow up.

As the Marines loaded up on the jet, Keith noticed something. Sergeant Martin, the first Marine to actually see Saven, was staring at Keith from beside a row of boxes being loaded in the jet.

Martin looked emotionally disturbed.

Keith approached him, sticking his hand out to shake it. "Well, another Crucible down." Keith smiled.

"Yeah," Martin said. He faked a smile up at Keith, but looked down, and refused to shake his hand. He appeared to be holding something back.

"So what are your plans when you get back?" Keith asked.

"Are you serious?" Martin said, raising his eyebrows. Keith shook his head slightly, confused by Martin's answer.

"Keith, you do realize Belmont is still going to be my superior, right? If we would have won, that meant the rank of Major for Belmont, but importantly for me, a transfer," Martin explained. "Not anymore. That's just a dream."

"Uh, Martin. Man, I hate to hear that. The last thing I would have ever wanted is to see you continue to take his shit."

"See, you already knew, how?" Martin asked.

"I just do. He constantly hounds you. You're a sergeant but he treats you like a private. Just an observation."

Martin nodded, pulling out a cigarette. He lit it up and took a big draw. "You want one?"

"Ha. Nah, I'm good," Keith said.

"Yeah, it's against regulations in my unit, but I don't really give a shit right now."

"Well, hey, listen, I've got to get going, but I'm sorry if Saven startled you during the drill. We designed him—"

"Startled?" Martin interrupted.

"Well, I'm not saying you were afraid, I just mean—"

"I was… terrified," Martin interrupted again, tapering off his voice when he realized he might alert someone.

"I'm sorry, Martin. I didn't mean—"

"I had some of the most vivid nightmares in my entire life last night."

"Well again, that wasn't my intention either."

"I know, Keith. I'm not busting your balls, man."

Martin stepped in close to Keith, looking him dead in the eyes. He glanced over toward Belmont for a moment before speaking. "I want that."

"What?"

"I want that power to drive fear into my enemies. I want to be able to do that to people that deserve it."

"What do you mean? I don't—"

"*Stop* with the bullshit. I know that's a man under there, or part man. I want that, too. I want to feel the power that thing has." Martin explained.

"Martin, I think you're underestimating the power of artificial intelligence."

"No. No, I'm not. Listen, it's fine if you can't say anything, but you're talking to a Marine that has made a career out of killing drones with artificial intelligence for years. That thing is not AI."

Keith looked away. He wasn't the best liar, but he couldn't say anything.

"That's no drone," Martin insisted.

Even if SolarSystems ever wanted another ECHO unit, it wouldn't be Sergeant Martin. He was a good Marine, but not even close to the caliber of soldier needed for the program.

"Hey, Keith, you good?" Lucas hollered over at him.

"Yeah. I'll be right over."

Martin gave Keith a piercing gaze before he ran away. "Think about it, man. I'm perfect for it."

"Let's rock and roll!" Belmont barked. The Marines loaded up on their jet.

Keith stared at Martin, but didn't say a word.

Lucas closely watched Martin walk away as Keith caught back up to him. Martin stared back at them one last time before entering the jet, walking past Belmont on the rear gate.

"What was that about? That guy looks ill. Has he eaten since we've been here?" Lucas asked.

"He just asked me if he could be an ECHO," Keith said.

Lucas stopped him. "Wait, what?"

"I know. I have no idea how he knows for sure, but he does," Keith said.

"Wait, isn't that the guy Belmont shot in the chair?" Lucas asked.

"Yeah."

Suddenly, everyone's attention shifted to the exit. Two SolarSystems technicians in lab coats appeared. They were guiding Saven's pod on a mechanized dolly. Keith ran around it, making sure all his connectors were in place for the short flight back.

The Marines' jet was parallel to Keith's. Belmont's eyes followed Saven's pod until it was out of view. He shook his head side to side, squinting his eyes. He smashed the rear gate button with his hand, closing it. A minute later, the

Marines took off, blasting into the atmosphere and out of view.

"Looks good... Load him up," Keith said, giving them the thumbs up. He and his small staff ushered the pod up and strapped it in. Lucas followed in just behind them.

The pilot's voice came over the intercom. "Ladies and gentlemen, I'd like to have this bird off the ground in the next ten minutes, if possible. Storm's intensifying," he said in a calm, but commanding voice.

"Sure thing," Keith said. "I think we have everything loaded, but let me go back and double check." He had a little pop to his step, exiting the jet, thrilled about SolarSystems' first win.

"We'll be here," Lucas said, smiling.

Keith ran back to his control room one last time. The pilot was right. The storm was picking up. He didn't forget anything, so he dashed back toward the jet in the blizzard. He could hear the pilot throttling the solar-powered engines, keeping them warm as Keith darted across the courtyard.

He stepped onto the rear metallic lift gate. "Okay, we're good!" Keith rubbed his hands together excitedly while walking toward his seat.

"Damn, that's cold," Keith said. He hit the rear gate button.

"I think we need to talk." Lucas threw an arm over his seat, but noticed something behind him.

"Whoa, hold up, Keith. Who's that?" Lucas perked up and pointed out the back gate.

Keith turned around and saw a female in a thick white cloak. Her face was covered in a dark mask under a hood, and only her eyes were showing. She was standing in the snow about forty meters away from the jet. Somehow, he hadn't seen her earlier.

"That's not one of Casser's people?" Keith turned toward Lucas in confusion.

"I don't remember her. Either way, Casser is gone. Actually, everyone is. Go see what she's doing," Lucas said in a concerned voice.

Confused, Keith trudged back out a few feet into the blizzard. "Who are you with?" He raised his voice even louder. "Did you miss your flight?"

The female stayed silent.

Keith stepped closer until he was within a few feet of her. He could tell something about her was unusual. Her clothing and disposition were out of place. "Ma'am, it's cold. You can't be out here. You with Casser?" Keith asked again, raising his voice slightly in the blizzard.

The woman turned her head, looking out into the distance. "I'm with Michael," she responded.

"W-What did you just say?" Keith replied. His eyes widened, and he took a step back.

"Are you Lucas Anderson?" she asked.

Suddenly, the woman stepped closer, coming eye to eye with Keith. "Does the name Michael Keller mean anything to you?" she questioned, yanking out a small submachine gun. She pointed it at Keith's stomach. "It means *a lot* to me," she said, raising her voice.

"Where. Is. Michael?" she demanded.

Keith's mouth dropped as his bottom lip quivered. He glanced behind him toward Lucas, feeling his heart pounding inside his chest.

"Don't look back again or I'll fill your gut with lead. Don't make me prove how little I care about your life."

"You're *her*..." Keith whispered.

She dropped her hood, revealing an unnaturally beautiful red headed woman with red eyes of scorn. But suddenly, that changed. Her hair turned to a dirty blonde and her eyes changed to green. More wrinkles appeared on her face and she looked more natural, less perfect.

Vala.

Her eyes stood out most of all. They reminded Keith of himself during a period of his own life. A time of despair, loss, anger, and madness. Even though her eyes were green now, they didn't look any less like fire.

"Y-You're Michael's, how did you? Find him?" Keith said under his breath. It sounded like he wanted to cry. Some of it was fear, but most of it was empathy in remembering his own experience.

"Where is he?!" She poked the machine gun barrel into his stomach hard, forcing him to hunch over.

"Ohhh!" Keith keeled over. Saliva streamed from his mouth. He couldn't believe this was happening. "Nooooo," Keith said. He knew there was no absolution for her, much like himself all those years ago when he looked into one of the hospital staff's eyes, begging them to let his pregnant wife in.

They couldn't help him, and now, he couldn't help her.

Lucas immediately stood up from inside the jet, looking out at Keith. He had to know something was very wrong. He could now see the gun, unobscured by Keith's body as he hunched over.

"Stand up!" She barked at Keith. Lucas darted out of jet with a gun drawn on her. "Tell the pilot to contact command. We have a security situation!" Lucas yelled back to one of the crewmembers.

"Yes, sir!" the crewmember replied.

Keith couldn't stand. Vala snatched him up off the ground, pulling his 190-pound frame up with ease. His feet came off the ground a couple of inches.

"Aaaarrrghhh—Lucas!" Keith doubled over as she twisted his body around awkwardly, pointing the gun at his head, using him as a shield.

"So that's Lucas, huh?" she said. She placed Keith directly in front of herself, giving Lucas no room to take a shot.

"You have Michael, don't you?" she said.

"Put the gun down!" Lucas ordered.

"I'm only here for one thing, and if I don't get it, people are going to die," she said.

"Ma'am, I don't know what this is, but you need to release him!" Lucas demanded loudly and clearly. His tone was focused, but calm, as his blue eyes honed in on Vala. The snow pelted his face, but he never blinked once.

"Michael Keller!" She shoved the hot gun barrel against Keith's temple. "I know he's here, and I know *you* have him!"

Behind Lucas was her Michael, but he wasn't who she remembered. Lucas bit his bottom lip hard, glaring right at Keith.

"Ma'am, there is *no* scenario where this ends well unless you put the gun—"

"Tell you what. You give me Michael, and you can have your buddy here. I'll trade you," she said.

Lucas glared back at the pod, then at Vala. He pitched his eyebrows forward, breathing slowly. Keith could tell he was lining up a shot, but so could Vala.

Lucas fired. The bullet struck her gun's suppressor, knocking it from her hand. Vala hurled Keith toward Lucas, nearly knocking them both to the ground. Lucas expended several more rounds into the blizzard as she disappeared.

"Urrgggghh!" Keith smacked face-first into the snow.

Lucas probed for a shot, but nothing was there. "Get inside!" Lucas yelled with his gun drawn as Keith crawled forward. The crewmembers helped him back onboard.

"Go! We're clear. Everyone is onboard. Get us out of—" Lucas pounded on the deck in the direction of the pilot's cabin.

"Hold on!" The pilot whooped over the intercom, realizing the urgency of the situation.

The G-force pinned them down. "Everyone all right?" Lucas rocked back and forth, but was still in command of the situation.

"I'm fine," Keith said.

"How did she know my name?" Lucas asked, panning around.

"I-I don't know," Keith responded.

Keith felt like an accomplice in someone else's madness. The madness he endured in his own struggle was one thing. Now he had assisted in someone else's. He didn't blame her. He was shocked at her tenacity. But deep down, he understood her pain.

"We've got a tremendous problem, Keith. I know you understand that," Lucas said in a low voice as the jet leveled out at cruising speed.

Keith stared out the window at a loss for words.

"Just so I'm sure, this is crazy, that *was* the woman from Saven's human life, right? His wife or?" Lucas asked, breathing heavily.

"Yes, *Vala*, his fiancée," Keith said. Suddenly, that name being spoken triggered something. A knocking sound was heard. Everyone's eyes moved to it. It was coming from Saven's pod. It got louder and louder.

"Okay, *now* what?" Lucas questioned.

Keith hurried over toward the stasis pod and looked inside. Saven was smashing his head against the bulletproof glass, violently attempting to bash through it as the jet lifted high into the atmosphere. Each impact was harder than the last, knocking the pod back and forth.

"What?! What's it doing?" Lucas asked as he rushed over to the pod.

"I don't know! I've got to shut him—"

Suddenly, Saven's metallic hand broke through the glass, grabbing Lucas by the collar. "Aaahhh-hhhhhh!" he cried as Saven slammed Lucas' face against the glass.

"Turn it off!!" Lucas attempted to push himself away from the ECHO's grasp.

Saven opened his mouth, exposing his huge fangs. He gnawed at the glass that Lucas' forehead pressed against. Saven made a loud screeching noise, unlike anything Keith had ever heard. The crewmembers froze. Some placed their hands over their ears and huddled down in their seats.

"Stop it!" One of the crewmembers screamed.

"What's going on!?" The copilot ran out of the cabin.

Saven continued bashing his head against the glass as it began to crack.

"I got it!" Keith pressed a series of commands on the pod's control panel, sedating Saven. Lucas felt his grip loosen, yet he still had to pry each individual finger off his collar with both hands, using his body weight to get free.

Lucas gasped loudly, panting. "He's...still...moving." Lucas examined his head as it bobbed back and forth.

"The sedation should be setting in—"

BOOOM! A shotgun-like sound erupted. Shrapnel from the pod shattered outward as Saven's metallic wings unfolded. Keith covered his face with his hands. The force from the blast knocked Lucas between a row of seats.

"God! No!" Keith yelled. A blur darted toward the rear gate, punching a hole through it. Oxygen masks dropped from the ceiling as the cabin lost pressure. A loud roar enveloped the cabin from the engine and wind.

"Oh God!"

"Masks!" Lucas held on as the pilot attempted to regain control. A siren blared as red lights strobed inside the cabin. Then, a secondary shield door cascaded, instantly muting them off from the open air.

"No. No. No," Keith said, running toward the gate. He looked out the window.

Lucas grabbed him, tossing him into his seat. "He's gone! GONE!"

"How? I-I don't know how that—"

"You're in shock. Concentrate Keith. Can you shut him down remotely?" Lucas asked.

"Yes, I... What just happened? Ahhh. Let me think... He's gliding. I need to give him some time to land. I can't shut him down at twenty thousand feet," Keith said, looking out the window. His face was red.

"He almost killed me," Lucas said.

"Look at the door, Lucas. All of us could be dead if he wanted." Keith said.

The copilot ran back into the cabin, assessing the rear gate. "Situation report. Now!" he demanded.

"As of a few moments ago, the most dangerous weapon man has ever created is out in the wild. Swing back around so we can retrieve him," Keith explained.

"What? Absolutely not," the copilot said.

"I'll shut him down completely!" Keith said.

"You've just proven you can't control it. No way in hell I'm putting us in jeopardy again without supporting units. You may be in operational control of your prototype, but we're in charge of this aircraft. Sit down, strap in, and shut your damn mouth until we land!" The copilot ordered, pointing at Keith.

"Turn it around! Now!" Keith stood up, pointing back at the co-pilot as he slowly backed away. He turned, quickly stepping back toward the cabin. "Not going to happen!" The copilot said with his back turned.

"I have to make this right," Keith said, shaking his head in shock.

Lucas kneeled down, picking up a fragment from the destroyed pod. He stared at it for a few moments, shaking his head.

"So your prototype is an artist?" Lucas said.

"What?" Keith snapped around. Lucas showed Keith the debris, exposing an image of a female's face.

"Not the best portrait I'm sure, but that looks a lot like the woman that just tried to kill us." Lucas observed, pitching Keith the piece of metal.

"It's her, no doubt about it now." Keith examined the likeness.

".... You knew?" Lucas asked.

"I saw it earlier, I just... I didn't believe, I don't know," Keith replied.

"You were told her memories were erased, but maybe... some *other* power is at work here, something we're unaware of?" Lucas suggested.

Keith shook his head side to side. His eyes danced around the plane. Lucas put his hand on Keith's shoulder, comforting him.

"The way I see it now, this project was designed to fail. Soon as we land, we'll head right back and pick him up, I'll call in a transport jet now, and we'll handle it before Amery finds out. Whatever you need. Don't worry about your career if they threaten you. You have a career waiting for you." Lucas whispered. "You did more than enough here."

"But there's one more thing I can do." Keith nodded his head slowly.

"What's that?" Lucas asked.

"I want to go to them personally, no weapons," Keith said.

"That's not the best strategy." Lucas said, raising his eyebrows. Keith stared into the distance for several moments in deep thought.

"Maybe not. But for once in a long while an opportunity has presented itself to me," Keith explained. Lucas sighed loudly, glancing up for a moment.

"You know, I'm not sure what you're suggesting here. If it's what I think, it sounds crazy. But, so does the alternative. If we pull Saven away from her again, she'll just hunt him down, putting everyone at risk. It's one hell of a tough call."

"Not for me," Keith said.

"But, let's think, it could be *you* who's in the most danger when you confront her alone?" Lucas raised his eyebrows.

"I'm willing to risk it for what I have to do."

Chapter Sixteen

Vala fell down on her knees before collapsing face first into the snow, breathing heavily. She paused for a few moments, but then the tears came. She yearned for Michael—his warmth, his touch, his voice, his smell. Things no one could replace and only she could understand.

She screamed in a haunting voice. She felt extreme, excruciating pain, like ripping an arrowhead back through someone's heart. Her soul was in agony. Now, the torturous path of sorrow would be resurrected from her hope. Subconsciously, she altered her tears just as she could the color of her skin or hair. Blood red tears soaked the pure white snow beneath her.

She looked up at the heavens, weeping loudly as the sun came up. She rubbed her eyes. Something was slowly falling toward her, eclipsing part of the sun. It looked like an angel. A dark, shining angel with huge wings, slowly drifting towards her.

She stretched out her arms toward it. "H-Help me… please. I can't do it anymore," she pleaded.

The figure grew larger and larger until it landed right in front of her. She buried her face in her lap, then looked up, her eyes soaked with red tears. The silhouetted figure slowly held out its arms. It touched her hands, softly pressing its cold, metallic fingers between hers.

She knew it was *him*.

"Mike?" she whispered, pulling herself toward him, but she collapsed.

Before she could fall, he scooped her up in his arms as the snow fell. He extended his metallic wings, encasing her inside a shard cocoon with him.

"It's you. W-what have they...done?" she said softly, cupping her hand along his jaw.

Her eyes cleared instantly. She could see him. She ran her fingers across his mask. "One last mission you told me, you told me you had one more," she said.

Michael touched his metallic forehead to hers, squeezing her tightly. Vala closed her eyes. Then, she let out a long shuddering sigh that seemed to resonate relief from the depths of her soul. They embraced one another without a word, protected inside his wings.

***

A jet rumbled in the distance as they held each other. Michael began to lose consciousness from the lingering sedation.

"No matter what happens next..." Vala said.

Michael opened his mouth, attempting to sound out the words, but he couldn't.

"...I know, you love me," she said.

They could see the jet land out in the distance. A male figure exited the rear gate, approaching with his hood over his head. He battled the wind as he trudged through the snow towards them. As he grew closer, Vala stood up to confront him, but Saven pulled at her wrist. The man removed his hood. It was Keith.

"That's far enough!" Vala yelled. She could see Keith's breath puff faster and faster in the cold air.

Saven tried to stand. Vala dipped under his arm, helping him to his feet. They hobbled forward slowly toward Keith until they stopped right in front of him.

Keith took his hands out of his pockets.

"Slowly!" Vala yelled. In one hand, Keith held the piece of metal. It was the portrait of Vala that Michael chiseled into his pod. Keith held it out so she could see it. She glanced at Michael then back at Keith.

***

Five months later...

Dr. Amery growled at the TV. A handsome, ethnically ambiguous news anchor smiled out to viewers from a news station. His coiffed dark hair and sharp navy suit were hollywood perfect under the robot-controlled lighting.

"Welcome. My name is Aaron Wallace with a special BBC news report. Sources in the Americas reported that corporate juggernaut *SolarSystems* has been attacked by what the United States is calling terrorists. However, no causalities have been reported. Sources indicated that the attackers broke in and destroyed archives within the research and development facility. The total cost of this attack has yet to be determined, but Dr. Richard Amery, the company's founder and CEO suggested his military weapons division took a substantial blow, sending him back to day zero. Amery said the attackers also left a personal message to him, however he would not comment on it specifically. This attack comes only months after Amery's lead scientist, Keith Sanders strangely disappeared after a weapons test in Alaska. More on this developing story to come."

Dr. Amery muted the audio, pulling back his hair. Just outside his office voices could be heard. "Sir, we'll need that letter they left for evidence." A Federal agent peered around the door at Amery.

"It's addressed to me, so give me a moment to read it first. Can I have that moment? Please?" Amery said. He sighed loudly.

"Technically I don't have to, it's evidence, but I'll give you a couple of minutes." The agent said, he exited the room, leaving Amery alone. Amery stared at the yellow envelope for a few seconds, then snatched it off the desk. He read the address line. *To: Dr. Richard Amery, architect of the ECHO project.* He tore into it, raccoon style.

Dr. Amery,

By now, you understand I know everything. I've had access to your files for weeks. I've seen all the sensitive files regarding the ECHO project, and I'm baffled.

I know you used me to run your Star Rust contracts. I know Lucas was the competition and you wanted him gone. That's why you led me to Alaska. You hoped I would react violently.

Sorry to disappoint.

Unfortunately, that's only the beginning of your scheme. I know you used Michael. You left my memory inside him to fortify his ambition. You left him to live inside an infinite wheel of torture, giving him just enough hope that his success as a military pawn would someday be rewarded. A reward that would have never come.

So, how could I react nonviolently here? After some thought, I think you value love. I really do. You understand the power that it has to propel people forward. You've used it to your advantage. The only difference is, you don't love people. No. You love wealth.

My mission now is to make all your competitors successful with the knowledge I've gained from your research, especially Lucas. You have some exciting projects that I'm sure they'll love. Things that could improve humanity.

Your bread and butter, your ultra-sensitive solar technology, will now be available for the world to use, not just the US military. Those heavily guarded schematics you gained from Star Rust are now online. I think that will make the world a better place, don't you agree?

The ECHO project. This was difficult. It's very personal, as you can imagine. I had a few different ideas, but I think you'll like the one I've chosen. In your files, all the government officials you pitched the ECHO project to were under the impression that Michael was an artificial intelligence unit. That's clever. Why would you need them to think that, Doctor? Perhaps it was unethical? You even removed his ability to speak, just in case. To clear the air, I'm going to wait until I think you've had time to read this letter, then I'm going to forward the ECHO project files to the Department of Defense, as well as the FBI. I'm sure they'll help you sort it out.

My goal here was not to endanger your life, but in saying that, consider yourself lucky to be alive. Someone you know taught me how to deal with my anger, with purpose.

I want you to see your toy box burn. I want you to watch the only thing you love fall apart from behind bars, while all your competitors succeed.

Despite what has been done to Mike, you left us enough information to reverse much of it with the right doctors. We've already started the process. He'll never be the same, but none of us will be. What's important is that we're together.

I'll leave you to enjoy the show. I'm sure your stockholders will be in for quite a ride after today.

Sincerely, Vala Thomas Keller.

Amery stood up slowly, his fists shaking. He leaned on his desk, closing his eyes. Amery could hear voices out in the hall, one was particularly loud. "Is Amery still in his office?!"

"Yes, he was a couple minutes ago. Why?" Another voice answered.

"Detain him. Get in there and put him in cuffs! Now!"

Four agents busted into the office, headed for Amery. Amery reached under his desk, he grabbed a pistol, pointing it inside his mouth. "Whoa! No! Don't!" One of the agents yelled. Amery shook his head side to side. He glanced at the agents in front of him, they begged him to put the gun down. However, one of them, a female was quiet. Her face was emotionless, a cold, blank stare.

BAM! As sudden and loud as the gunshot was, silence blanketed the room and hallway immediately after. Everyone stared in shock. Blood splattered the wall behind Amery. His body fell back against the wall and his head slumped over.

"Dammit!"

"Shot fired!"

Several other agents crammed inside the room to see what happened. "Clear, we're clear. My god... Get a cleanup crew in here, everyone stay away from that side of the office! What the hell!? What just happened?"

"He said he was going to read the letter, he just told me he needed a minute," the young male agent said, he appeared shocked. His eyes danced around in confusion.

The female agent continued staring at the body for several seconds, then she slowly backed out of the room and down the hall. She glided out of the building, through the slew of reporters, ignoring them as they badgered her for answers.

"Ma'am, Ma'am, can you comment on what just happened, we think we heard a gunshot?" A tall, lanky male reporter ran her down. He stood in front of her, blocking her path.

"Out. Of. The. Way." She said, staring a hole through him.

She started down a large flight of stairs that leveled out in an expansive concrete plain. The middle area showcased a giant logo, beautifully crafted in marble that read *SolarSystems*. Underneath the logo in smaller text read, "*The future, now.*"

She stared down the logo as she passed by it. She shook her head side to side slowly.

She walked far out into the parking lot and took off her FBI jacket, dropping it on the ground. She got inside a red, solar powered Audi SUV with tinted windows, starting the engine. "We're clear." She said. Her hair slowly changed from a jet black to a dirty blonde. Her eyes turned from a dark brown to green. A man in the back seat slowly leaned forward with a baseball cap covering part of his face. "Did,

did, h-he read the letter?" The man asked, he struggled with his words.

"Yes baby," she said softly. She turned around, kissing the man. His face was severely deformed. She smiled at him, staring deep into his eyes with love. He stared back, nodding his head slowly.

"It's o-over then," he said.

"It's over Michael." Vala murmured.

She accelerated forward through the gate. She glanced through the rear-view mirror at Michael in the back seat. He spun around, staring out towards the Solarsystems' logo until it disappeared from view. He turned back, exposing his face full of tears. He glared up at her in the mirror and let out a long sigh. He reached his metallic hand forward as it shook, grabbing Vala's. He squeezed her hand tightly. Tears streamed down her face too, but this time, the tears slid   down   around   a   smile.

Epilogue

"You know, Keith, eventually you'll have to return to civilization. They'll wanna know your side of the story." Lucas clapped him on the shoulder. He stood parallel to Keith as they stared out into a large warehouse from an office. Keith sported a lab coat with a tablet in his hand.

"I've got enough work here with you for a lifetime," Keith said, glancing down at his tablet.

"Well—"

"Not saying I'm staying forever, but I'm not going anywhere for a little while anyway," Keith interrupted. He had a smirk on his face. Lucas chuckled under his breath.

"So long as you give your two weeks' notice."

"Absolutely. I wouldn't want to put you in a bad position with trillions of dollars' worth of technology laying around here."

"You might. So, any plans when you leave?" Lucas asked.

"Not exactly, but I'm not going to work as much."

"You're working much less here than you did at SolarSystems I thought?" Lucas asked.

"Yeah. You're right, but I'm going to take an ordinary job back home in Minnesota. Something less cutting edge, I think."

Lucas scratched his chin with his tablet. "You know I'll support you no matter what you do. You've given us a tremendous boost in our research since you've been here."

"Thanks. I wish I would have worked with you from the beginning. I wasn't in my normal frame of mind when I worked on the ECHO project," Keith said. Lucas bobbed his head slowly.

"Not to intrude, but what's giving you such clarity now? You seem like a new man the last few months," Lucas noted. Keith turned his head and smiled. He paused for several seconds as his thoughts seemed to drift a million miles away.

"That day, out there in the snow with Michael and Vala. I've thought about it a lot," Keith said.

"It's crossed my mind several times as well," Lucas replied.

"You know what I keep going back to?" Keith asked.

"Hmm?"

"Every fiber in their bodies, mutated or augmented, was existing for the other. It was that magnetic connection, one that billions of dollars of tech couldn't even separate. It wasn't overnight, but I realize that life, *life* is worth living for that, even for just the chance at it. Whether to fight tooth and nail to get it back, or start all over again from scratch. I know now it's worth it," Keith explained. Lucas nodded his head slowly.

"You and I have never discussed our pasts. I like it that way Keith. But, I know what happened to your wife. My view is that while Saven helped you forget, *Michael* helped you remember. All this obsession with dominance, wealth, and technology, it's just *noise* and means little in comparison to what Michael and Vala have, and to what you will have, again."

Thank you for reading! I hope you enjoyed my little tale. Please don't forget to give this book a quick review. Even just a two word, "Liked it" or "Hated it" review helps so much. Positive or negative, I am grateful for all feedback from my readers.

Sign up to Receive Free Books and $0.99 New Releases at www.enterechoeffect.com

For every new book release, I randomly select 200 mailing list subscribers to receive a free advance Kindle copy. All other subscribers will receive a special offer to purchase the book for only $0.99 on the day of release, before the price goes up to $3.99. This is not a newsletter. You will only be contacted about free books and $0.99 discounts on New Releases. Thanks again for your support!

For updates or to contact the author, visit: www.enterechoeffect.com

About the Author

Robert Armstrong is a former intelligence analyst with a passion for creativity and science. With degrees in Social Science and Medical Sleep Disorders, he prides himself in understanding what makes the human brain tick, both day and night, the link between the subconscious and conscious.